January's Betrayal

A Larry Macklin Mystery-Book 3

A. E. Howe

Books in the Larry Macklin Mystery Series:

November's Past (Book 1)

December's Secrets (Book 2)

January's Betrayal (Book 3)

February's Regrets (Book 4)

March's Luck (Book 5)

April's Desires (Book 6)

May's Danger (Book 7)

Copyright © 2016 A. E Howe

ISBN: 0-9862733-2-5
ISBN-13: 978-0-9862733-2-2

DEDICATION

For Daisy, the petite tabby cat who is the inspiration for Ivy. In order to preserve her cushy life, she has dedicated herself to supervising my writing efforts. She's convinced that I would not be able to write a single word without her help. Who knows, maybe she's right!

CHAPTER ONE

It was after midnight and cold. The first thing I saw when I pulled up behind the shopping center didn't make me feel better. Held back by crime scene tape were two news vans and my dad's pickup truck. As an investigator, the last things you want at your crime scene are reporters and the sheriff. And when the sheriff is also your father, you're doubly screwed.

On the other side of the tape, two of our patrol cars were parked at odd angles, all their lights on and illuminating the bodies of a man and a woman. As I parked my unmarked car, the crime scene van pulled up next to me. Shantel Williams and Marcus Brown, two of our best techs, got out and greeted me.

"None of this is good," Shantel said, carrying her box of equipment.

"I was told Nichols shot a suspect?"

"Not the half of it. He shot Ayers."

"Jeffrey Ayers, the suspect in the rapes?"

"That's what Marti in dispatch said," Marcus responded.

As we approached the scene, I could see my father staring at the bodies from a distance. He heard us coming and held up the crime scene tape so that Marcus and Shantel could go under. They set their boxes down and started removing their cameras.

Dad pulled me aside. Behind him, the news crews were already testing their lights and microphones.

"This is going to go political fast," he said, his voice low and ominous.

"What the hell happened?"

"That's what we're going to have to figure out. Look, I know you're on call tonight, but I'm going to need to assign another investigator as the lead."

"Because of Ayers?"

Jeffrey Ayers had been our chief suspect in a series of rapes. But as we dug deeper, the evidence pointed away from him and two days ago Dad had announced that Ayers was no longer considered a suspect.

Dad nodded to the news vans. "Press is already on top of the story. I have to be above this. If Ayers raped and killed this woman then I'm in big trouble. It's not going to help if it looks like I put my son in charge of the investigation. Perception is going to be almost as important as the reality."

"I understand."

"That doesn't mean I don't want you involved. This coming on the heels of what you told me about Matt…" He shrugged. "I'm not feeling very comfortable. You know Matt would have been my second choice."

Dad seemed to have aged ten years in the last month. Before Christmas I'd stumbled upon a situation suggesting that Matt Greene, one of the best investigators in our department and a horse's ass, was also a dirty cop.

A gust of wind from the north sent a chill through me. "What do you want me to do?" I asked quietly.

"I called Pete in. I'm going to give him the lead. He works well with Sam in internal. Sam's going to be handling the use-of-force report on Nichols."

"And since Pete and I work as partners most of the time…"

"It will seem natural that you're close to the case. Of

course, Matt will still have to be involved a bit since he took the lead in the second rape."

"What a mess," I said, shaking my head.

Another car pulled up next to the crime scene van and Pete Henley's large bulk emerged. He looked around for a minute before he spotted us and came over. In his mid-forties and a little over three hundred pounds, with a wife and two teenage daughters that were the center of his world, Pete's easygoing nature fooled a lot of people. But he was a natural investigator and the best shot in the department.

In Adams County, Pete was the man with his ear to the ground. He knew everybody in our small, rural north Florida county. For most families, he could tell you their history going back for as many generations as they'd lived here. He was also well tuned into local politics, so he didn't need to have the pitfalls of the current situation spelled out for him.

Dad told Pete he was the lead investigator and filled him in on what little information he had.

"I'm on it," Pete said with reluctance. He turned and walked over to the crime scene tape, lifting it up, and awkwardly slipped under it.

"Go on," Dad said to me, looking over at the news crews who were done shooting background footage of the scene and were heading toward us. I avoided making eye contact with the reporters as I hurried under the tape.

The bodies were located at the back of a small shopping center. The woman's body was half hidden behind a dumpster near a loading dock. Five feet away was the man's body, curled up and face down on the pavement. I never would have recognized him as Ayers. Marcus and Shantel were methodically taking pictures from different angles.

"Do we know her name?" Pete asked Deputy Julio Ortiz, who was standing well back from the bodies.

"She is… was Angie Maitland. I went to school with her."

Julio was about five years younger than me, twenty-five maybe. Around the sheriff's office he was always hanging

7

out with the clowns, the guys that razzed each other, came up with silly practical jokes and challenged each other to weightlifting or running contests. There were no jokes tonight, though, his voice sad and dismayed. In a small county like ours, you realized pretty early that the car wreck you responded to or the domestic disturbance call you answered might involve someone you knew. It made a hard job harder. And was one of the reasons I'd rather have been doing something else.

"Has her family been informed?" Pete asked.

"I don't know."

Pete pulled out his radio and checked with dispatch. No one had contacted the family. "Would you to do it?" Pete asked Julio.

"Sure," Julio nodded, turning away to get the address from dispatch.

"What about Ayers?" I asked Pete.

"We'd better do it. We'll go over after we talk with Nichols."

Pete watched Marcus and Shantel work for another couple of minutes. "Hold up, guys," he said when they both lowered their cameras for a moment.

Pete turned and shouted to the other deputies standing around, "Turn off all the headlights for a couple minutes!" It took a second for everyone to process what he'd said, but slowly two of them went to the cars and turned off the lights.

"Take some pictures," he told the vague shadows of Marcus and Shantel.

It was very dark behind the store with the headlights off. Streetlights glowed in the distance, but that just seemed to amplify the darkness near the loading dock.

After a minute Pete shouted, "Nichols, turn on your lights!" The headlights of a car parked fifty feet away came on, illuminating the bodies while casting stark shadows against the back wall of the building. Pete asked Marcus and Shantel for a few more pictures, then finally shouted for everyone to turn the lights back on.

"Let's go talk with Nichols," he said to me.

I followed him over to where Deputy Isaac Nichols leaned against his patrol car. First thing I noticed was that his holster was empty.

"They already bagged it," he said when he saw us looking at his holster.

"Don't think you have much to worry about," Pete responded.

"I know it's standard procedure, just like the suspension. Still hard to take," Nichols said mournfully. "I just wished I'd gotten here in time to save her. I damn sure don't regret shooting him."

Pete held up his hand. "Careful what you say. Breathe deep." I could see Nichols was still shaking from the adrenaline dump his system had received.

"You don't have to tell me. I'm not going to give my formal statement for a couple days."

This was the advice we all received during our training. Memory is notoriously unreliable right after a traumatic event, and actually becomes more accurate a couple days later. If you make a detailed statement right after a shooting, you're probably going to regret it. There will be details that don't fit and that you know to be wrong, but if you change your story then the damage is done and you risk being grilled by attorneys on both sides of the aisle during a trial.

"I don't want details right now. Just give me the rough outline of what went down," Pete requested.

"When I drove back here, I heard a scream and I saw the guy on top of the woman. I didn't know who he was. I got out and told him to get up. He didn't. I ran over toward them and all of a sudden he turned and came at me. I saw a knife in his hand. Pulled my gun and fired twice." There was a tremor in Nichols's voice. His hands twisted and kneaded each other. "I never thought I'd be the guy that had to shoot someone."

"Why'd you drive back here?" Pete asked the question

that had been upper-most in my mind.

"My field training officer showed me this spot. I've caught prostitutes, people doing drugs… Once I caught some guy that was dumping a couple purses he'd stolen." All of that could be checked easily.

Pete patted him on the back. "We'll get this cleared up. HR will set you up with someone to talk to."

"I don't know," Nichols said, answering some question that only he heard. "It's been a crazy night."

Pete and I walked away, not talking until we were out of his hearing. "They found a knife?" Pete asked me.

"I got here just a few minutes before you did. I didn't see one, but maybe it's under the body. Let's go find out."

As we walked back toward the bodies, I saw Dad standing under a floodlight as he was interviewed by one of the news crews from Tallahassee. His voice was loud and deep. "I take full responsibility for any decision made by my office."

Dad could irritate the crap out of me, but I'd never doubted his integrity or dedication to his job. After my mother died, Dad was lost without her, so I'd encouraged him to run for sheriff as a way to redirect his attention. He'd been a deputy for half his life and I knew there was no one in the county who could do a better job. Being sheriff saved him and did a lot to improve the lives of the people of Adams County.

I noticed the coroner's van had been added to the growing number of random vehicles arranged like vultures flocking to fresh roadkill. Marcus and Shantel were standing back, filming the body of Jeffrey Ayers as Dr. Darzi examined it. I was surprised to see him. Normally, his participation was limited to the actual autopsy. Dad must have called him personally. With an officer's career and Dad's reelection in the balance, it was vital that the investigation be above reproach.

Ayers's body was probed, measured and handled with detached professionalism, leaving no doubt that he was now more a piece of evidence than a person.

"Little help," Dr. Darzi said to no one in particular. Marcus went over and gave him a hand turning the body onto its side. Sure enough, there was a six-inch-long folding knife, blade out, lying underneath. Darzi examined the corpse's back. "Looks like one of the bullets went through him. The other probably broke up or is lodged against a bone or in an organ." We would have to look for the bullet that went through the body.

Shantel and Marcus moved in and emptied Ayers's pockets, bagging and tagging everything. Finally the body was lifted onto a gurney and moved to the coroner's van. Darzi then went over and began the same process with the woman's body.

"At least they found a knife," Pete said to me in a low voice. He hated the press and they were still hovering around, though they had enough respect for the victims to stay back and keep their cameras off the scene. The South had changed a lot, for both good and ill, but most of us still had some respect for the dead. It was a mix of superstition and awe brought on by being in the presence of the ultimate mystery.

"But did Ayers kill the woman?" I asked Pete.

"Not with a knife," Dr. Darzi answered. "There are no cuts on the body. She appears, only appears, mind you, to have been strangled." He probed around her neck and revealed a rope that had been pulled so tight that it was hidden under the flesh of her throat.

"I can't decide whether this is good or bad," Pete said. "Looks good for Nichols and bad for the sheriff." Pete looked around. "Where is Ayers's car?"

We went on a hunt for it and found it parked in front of the store. "That's odd. It's not parked in a space," I said.

"Not like anyone's going to complain." Pete indicated the empty lot. "Pretty strange he'd park out here and drag her around back."

"Maybe he saw her walking toward the back and

followed her."

We both shrugged. This early in the investigation, there were just too many questions.

We walked back to the scene and Pete told Shantel where the car was and that they'd need to process it tonight. It would be towed back to our small impound lot, a quarter acre of asphalt behind the sheriff's office with a ten-foot fence topped by concertina wire.

"Okay now, if you're going to start telling us how to do everything, you may as well have the B Team out here. You know you got the A Team, so let us do our thing." Shantel was always ready to throw around the banter. That and the fact she and Marcus were the best forensics team in north Florida were the main reasons we all liked working with them.

"I'd never think of telling you how to do your business," Pete said with a smile.

"You better not, big man, or you can get down here and crawl around on your hands and knees looking for God knows what," Shantel said as she moved around the bodies with her headlamp focused six inches in front of her, looking for anything that might turn out to be important trace evidence.

I turned to Pete. "We know how Ayers got here. It would help to know Angie Maitland's movements."

"Let's go tell Ayers's family what's happened. We've got time to figure out why Maitland was here," Pete said, and we headed for his car.

This was a different dynamic for us. Normally we'd split up and handle different tasks, then come back together and compare notes. But I think neither of us wanted to take the risk of missing something in a case this complicated. With ten months to go until the election, Dad's main opponent, Charles Maxwell, Calhoun's chief of police, was already campaigning heavily. He and Dad had never gotten along and Chief Maxwell was sure to use this case as ammunition.

No one likes to do notifications. There are a dozen different ways they can play out and few of them are good. I've known deputies that were attacked by family members and others that couldn't leave because they were afraid a friend or relative might hurt themselves.

Jeffrey Ayers had been in his mid-thirties, but still lived at home with his mother. Not that surprising these days. Hers was a one-story ranch-style house in a middle-class neighborhood north of Calhoun. All the windows were dark when we pulled into the driveway. Looking at my watch, it was almost one-thirty. I closed my door carefully when I got out of the car, so as not to disturb everyone in the neighborhood. But as soon as the door clicked shut, one dog after another started barking. What can you do?

Pete walked heavily up to the door and rang the bell. It took two more tries before the porch light came on and a voice from inside asked who we were. We produced names and badges, then the door was opened by a surprisingly young-looking woman. She didn't look a day over fifty, even after being woken in the middle of the night.

"What's happened?" she asked, holding the door open for us to come in. She was wearing a blue robe and kept smoothing her hair as though she wished that she could brush it. "Is Jeffrey all right?"

"I'm sorry," Pete said quietly.

"Oh, my God. What?" She looked like she was going to collapse, so I put my hand on her arm and eased her down onto a wingback chair.

"Mrs. Ayers, I'm sorry, but your son is dead," I said, not wanting to drag it out. She knew something horrible had happened so what good would it do to delay the inevitable?

"How?" she asked.

I didn't want to tell her, but I didn't seem to be able to stop myself. "One of our deputies shot him."

"What? Why? Why did you kill my son?" She was pounding her fists on the arms of the chair so hard that it rocked back and forth. I knew that she really wanted to be hitting us.

Pete seemed at a loss. "Our deputy reported that your son was assaulting a woman and, when he ordered him to stop, your son turned and charged. The deputy had to defend himself."

"Lies!" she screamed. "All of those lies you told about him. He never hurt anyone!" She stopped pounding the chair and brought her hands up in front of her.

I knew what was going to happen a nanosecond before she flew out of the chair and started flailing at me.

I just curled up and let her thump me with her fists. Pete tried to get in between us and deflect some of the blows.

"Please stop now," Pete said. "I'm investigating the shooting. If your son's death wasn't justified, I promise we'll set the record straight."

Mrs. Ayers landed a few more blows, but her strength was fading. Finally she dropped back into the chair and began to sob.

"Is there someone you could call?" I asked gently.

"I have to tell Wayne," she said and then began crying again. I vaguely remembered that Jeffrey Ayers had a brother.

"Is that your other son?"

"Yes," she said, trying to control her sobbing. "He didn't do it. Jeffrey, he was here the night that girl was attacked. I know that."

During an interview regarding one of the rapes, she had told us that she'd heard Ayers come home and hadn't heard him go out again. But she had also admitted it was possible she could have fallen asleep and not heard him go back out.

"Where is he?" she asked. Tears still rolled down her face, but her breathing was coming under control.

"We have to take his body to the… hospital for an autopsy. We want the truth as much as you do," Pete told her.

"I can't think. Go. I don't want you all here."

"Do you want us to call your son?" I asked.

"No, just get out. I'll call him. Go. You've done enough!" she shouted. We quietly made our escape.

CHAPTER TWO

I could have used a cup of coffee, but in Calhoun everything shut down after one in the morning. It was the county seat, but had only ten thousand residents. There were a lot of great things about small town life, but 24/7 service wasn't one of them.

Back at the crime scene we set to work helping to gather evidence or, more accurately, collecting a lot of trash that would probably prove unconnected. After two hours, Pete finally found the bullet that had passed through Ayers's body. He bagged it up for its trip to the state's crime lab. The Florida Department of Law Enforcement would be providing assistance on this case as they did for most major crimes in small counties.

Major Sam Parks arrived at the scene when we were nearly done. He was in charge of most of the administrative divisions within the department, including budget and human services, and he would be heading up the internal review of the shooting. Parks was a humorless curmudgeon, but was respected by the rank and file for his forty years of service. He had an accountant's nose for errors and was meticulous to a fault. I'd heard Dad bemoan Parks's imminent retirement on more than one occasion. Dad never had to worry about the budget or trouble with the department's certification while Parks was running things.

"Everything in hand?" Parks asked Pete.

"At first glance it looks clean. But we'll know more after the forensics come back."

"Yep. Keep me informed," Parks mumbled. "I'm sending Nichols home. Told him he'd be on paid leave until the final report. Be safe." He turned and strode back to his car.

"That man was old when I joined the department," Pete said, shaking his head.

Pete had had his own run-in with Parks several years ago when he failed to respond to a shooting while on break. He didn't technically do anything wrong and was let off with a couple days' suspension and a note in his file. It was hard on Pete and he beat himself up over it for a long time. I'd heard him say once that he should have been terminated over the incident. It didn't help that Matt Greene, a patrol deputy at the time, had been the one who was being shot at. He certainly hadn't forgiven Pete and definitely believed he should have been fired. It had been difficult working in the same office with the two of them, and had been made all that much worse in the last month since I'd discovered that Matt might be corrupt.

With the news crews finally gone, Dad was leaning against his truck, watching as everyone finished up at the scene. I walked over to him and his eyes met mine. His were lacking the normal spark of self confidence I was used to.

"Son."

I didn't know what to say and just shook my head.

"You don't have to say it. Everything looks like it went down the way Nichols claims."

"There's a lot more work to be done. You know that. And you had good reason for letting Ayers go."

"Yeah, I thought so. But it doesn't look good now."

The first rape had occurred just before Christmas. Pete was the lead. A week later there was another attack and Matt picked it up. Three days later, when the third woman was assaulted, we'd known there was a serial rapist at work.

"You formed the task force as soon as you realized the cases were related. There are a hell of a lot of departments that wouldn't have put it together that fast," I tried to reassure him.

"And I put myself in charge of the task force. I'm thinking that might have been a mistake." It was tough listening to him second-guess his decisions.

"You did it because you cared. I don't think it was a mistake. A case like that needs resources and a high profile. Those were the reasons you put yourself at the head of the investigation. And when the next two rapes happened, we were at the scenes fast and with a lot of manpower."

"But what did I miss?"

"I don't think we missed anything."

"If Ayers was our rapist then we must have missed something," he said angrily.

"We questioned him because he knew the first and third victims. But it's a small county; everyone knows everyone," I said.

"But we arrested him because his car matched the description of a car seen shortly after one of the attacks. Plus, he had a bruise on his face that the last victim said she could have given him." Dad wasn't going to let this go.

"And you *released* him because an ATM machine's CCTV image taken two hours before the attack showed that he already had the bruise, corroborating his story that he hit himself in the jaw with a piece of lumber."

"If only one of the women had seen him."

"But they didn't. Our mistake might have been arresting him too soon."

"Why couldn't we have found some trace evidence?"

"Because the rapist was very careful. Which brings us to that last bit of evidence we found after we arrested him."

"Don't remind me," Dad grimaced.

None of the victims' medical exams or rape kits recovered any pubic hair. After we arrested Ayers, a physical exam revealed that he shaved his pubic region. Everything seemed to fit.

"Damn it! I should have continued to hold him even without the bruise being evidence."

"You know the State Attorney wouldn't have brought charges without something more than his circumstantial lack of pubic hair. Ayers even had an alibi for one of the rapes."

"It was his mother," Dad reminded me dismissively.

"But once you threw out the bruise the alibi looked a lot stronger."

"Five rapes altogether and now a murder. Six women whose lives have been damaged or destroyed. And their families…"

"Dad, stop this. You made the right decisions. Remember my first year with the department, when I was chasing that stolen car? He hit another car and kept going and I stayed with him. I remember feeling so good when I finally ran him off the road and cuffed him. But then I found out that the woman in the car he'd hit lost her leg and almost died.

"Remember what you told me when I was giving myself a hard time for not stopping and helping her? You said that decisions, no matter how well thought out, always have a chance of being wrong. But that you can't let that destroy your ability to do your job. Well, I'm throwing that back at you. Go home. Mauser's probably losing sleep wondering where you are."

That made him smile a little. Mauser was Dad's one-hundred-and-ninety-pound, black-and-white monstrosity of a dog. Theoretically he was a Great Dane, but my money was on Angus bull.

"Fat chance," Dad snorted as he climbed into his truck. He gave me a small wave as he drove off.

"He's going to be under a hell of a lot of pressure," Pete said, walking up behind me.

CHAPTER THREE

I woke up the next morning with Ivy rubbing her head against my face. Since I'd rescued her from a life on the streets, the little tabby cat had taken charge of my schedule when I was at home. She frowned upon sleeping in late, regardless of the lack of sleep the night before. I got up and fed her breakfast before opening my iPad and checking out the morning news.

The *Tallahassee Democrat* had a front page story on the shooting. Not a surprise. "Sheriff Ted Macklin Takes Responsibility for Releasing Rapist" was the headline. Not great, but it could have been worse. For the most part, the story wasn't too damning. The local TV station websites each had a video of the interview with Dad. Overall the local news outlets were pretty friendly to law enforcement. They needed good relationships to ensure regular news feeds from the different law enforcement departments. And local news ratings were all about the blood. "If it bleeds, it leads" was gospel.

By eight o'clock I was in my car for the quick five-mile ride to town. One of the great things about living and working in a rural county was no morning traffic. Especially this morning. The first twenty-four hours after catching a major case are critical. Even though we had a pat explanation for all the bodies in this case, we couldn't take anything for granted. We couldn't delay starting the paperwork and setting the hounds onto any hot trails.

I knew that Pete wouldn't be at the office yet. His morning routine called for him to be at Winston's Grill for their breakfast specials. I decided to meet him there. Normally not my thing, but I wanted to hear what folks were saying. I took the last space in the back of the lot. Winston's made more money between seven and ten in the morning than they did the rest of the day. Pete's car was parked in his usual spot under a sweetgum tree that was leafless in the middle of January.

Someone who didn't know any better would think that Pete took a lot of liberties spending the first couple hours of each day at a restaurant eating breakfast and chatting with the locals, but the truth was that he learned more talking to the regulars at Winston's than most of our deputies could learn in a week going door to door or making cold calls. The old timers and blue-collar folks who ate breakfast there were the very ones who kept a sharp eye on what was going on in the county. Once they were full of Winston's jumbo pancakes or bacon scramble special, they'd lean back and talk about everything—which couples were stepping out on each other, whose son had wrecked his car for the third time or who was down on their luck. And Pete was always there to hear them.

He nodded when he saw me coming toward his table in the back corner of the dining room. Two old farmers sitting with him looked up at me. Their expressions went dark as they got up, nodded curtly and went back to their table.

"I didn't mean to spoil anyone's appetite," I told Pete.

He waved me to one of the chairs that the men had vacated as he finished chewing and swallowing a big bite of sausage biscuit. "They aren't feeling very kindly toward your dad this morning." He gestured in the direction of people reading papers and eating breakfast before checking his phone, which was sitting on the table. Pete was addicted to texting with his wife and daughters.

"We can't do much about that. Best we can do is tie this all up as quickly as possible."

Mary, the owners' daughter, came over with an order pad. "Can I get you something?" she asked me.

"Just a coffee to go."

"Good thing that's all. If you want more you'll have to get here before this big moose gets his order in." She smiled at Pete, who just nodded as he cut up his pancakes.

"I'm going to make sure the investigation's done right," he said to me after Mary left.

"Absolutely. You know that's what I meant."

"I do, actually. Have I ever told you how glad I am to be working for your dad? There's more than one corrupt sheriff out there."

"I know. Unfortunately, an honest mistake could turn this election against him."

As though summoned by the mention of the election, Dad's opponent came walking thorough the door. Chief Charles Maxwell had been in charge of the small force that made up Calhoun's police department for a dozen years. In November he had announced that he was going to challenge Dad in the upcoming election for sheriff. I hated to admit it, but Maxwell had a chance. There were less than thirty thousand residents in Adams County and Calhoun was by far the largest of the county's three communities, so almost everyone knew Maxwell. He had a good reputation for keeping a handle on crime in the city, even though we at the sheriff's department did most of the heavy lifting. We had more than three times as many officers as the city, so when there was a real crime we usually did the work. But people don't always understand how things are done, and Maxwell was always quick to step in and be there for the perp walk in front of the cameras.

Maxwell took off his sunglasses and looked around the diner. He had one of his toadies with him, who went to the opposite corner of the room and grabbed a table for them. I thought Maxwell would ignore us as he usually did, but apparently he was in the mood to show his ass. He made eye contact with me and, after a ten-second staring contest, headed over to our table. I felt a kick under the table from Pete, who knew my opinion of the blowhard chief.

"Well, mornin' boys," Maxwell said, using his best good ol' boy voice. It was particularly irritating because it was all a big put-on. Maxwell came from Orlando. He'd been on the force down there for about ten years before moving north with his wife, who had gotten a job at Florida State University as an assistant law professor.

He also enjoyed playing up the fact that he was close to six and a half feet tall. He leaned over and looked at us like we were kids in a lunch room. "Guess your dad barfed on the buffet table with this one. I wouldn't have let a rapist loose." This last was said loud enough for the whole restaurant to hear.

"Of course you never could have caught one in the first place," I said, equally loudly and earning a few snickers from our fellow diners.

Maxwell's face turned red as he leaned down close to me and said menacingly, "Your dad better get his act together. I want a little bit of a challenge this fall." Then he turned and walked away to sit with his toady in the corner.

"Ass," I said under my breath.

"You did good," Pete said as Mary brought my coffee. I thanked her and got up.

"I'm heading for the office. It should be quieter there." I dropped a five-dollar bill on the table and left Pete to finish his breakfast.

Before driving out of the parking lot I sent a text to my girlfriend, Cara Laursen. She worked as a vet tech for Dr. Barnhill, but I couldn't remember what her hours were today. Almost immediately my phone rang.

"Hey! I've got an hour before I have to be at work," she said perkily.

"Guess you haven't heard."

"What?"

I filled her in on the events of the previous night, and their possible political implications.

"Damn. Is there anything I can do?"

"See me tonight?"

"You got it."

At the sheriff's department I parked next to Matt's car, remembering the night last month that I'd spent staring at its rear tires. Of course I hadn't known it was his car at the time. I was hiding in the woods near the local industrial park, staking out a drug deal that was going down and trying to identify a possible dirty cop who was aiding the drug dealers. Or so my new confidential informant, Eddie, had suggested. The car had pulled in close to the spot where I was lying on the ground with my binoculars. I had guessed that it must be the crooked cop, keeping watch over the drug deal, but, alone and without backup, I couldn't make a move. Hampered by the dark, I tried to remember as many details of the car as I could. I was eventually able to identify it as Matt's.

When I finally shared my suspicions with Dad, we came up with a plan. It involved having an outside IT guy install a tracking device on Matt's department-issued laptop. Hopefully he'd keep it in his car most of the time, which would allow us to compare his movements with known drug dealers and their hangouts. We would have preferred to put a tracking device directly on his car, but since he was using his personal car for business it was a grey area as to whether we would need a warrant to do it. We didn't have anywhere near enough evidence for that. And Dad wanted to make damn sure that anything we got from the tracker could be used in court.

"No one else is to know for now," Dad said.

"But that's going to make it very difficult to keep Matt at

a safe distance," I argued.

"If he's guilty then there might be others, and we don't want to give them any warning. And if he's innocent, it would be unfair for us to undermine his reputation as a very good investigator."

So it was our little secret, and we were waiting and watching. It was unsettling to sit beside Matt almost every day, suspecting that he had a secret of his own that he was keeping from all of us. In my mind that secret could be summed up in one word: betrayal.

Now I entered the building and waved at the desk sergeant before passing through the set of inner doors that led to the criminal investigations department and, eventually, Dad's office. Before I reached my desk I heard a commotion and walked down the hall to see a man pacing outside of the sheriff's door.

"I want to see him, now!" yelled an agitated, blond-haired man.

"I can't let you go in there," Dad's assistant responded, sounding harried.

"I don't give a damn what you say."

I came up behind the man and cleared my throat loudly. "Can I help you?" I said firmly, using my best *I'm in charge here* voice.

The man turned around. He was a couple inches taller than me and wore a blue work shirt and jeans. His eyes were sunken and his face was red from a volatile mix of emotions.

"I want to see the sheriff. He let that killer loose!" he yelled at me, holding his large, calloused hands up in front of me, clearly more in frustration than as any real threat.

"And you are?"

"I'm Allen Maitland. Who the hell are you?"

Damn. Angie Maitland's husband. What a way to start the morning. "I'm Deputy Larry Macklin. Mr. Maitland, let's go over to the conference room. We need to ask you some questions."

"I don't want to answer any of your questions. What's

25

the use? Angie's dead because... Wait... Macklin? Are you related to the sheriff?" His eyes were slits and his face looked like it was ready to explode.

"I'm his son. And if you'll just let me ask you a few questions, I'll ask my father to come out and talk with you."

"You sons of bitches! How could you let that rapist go? What the hell were you people thinking?" I wouldn't have thought it was possible, but his face was getting even redder. His hands went up again and I prepared myself to take him down if I had to.

"Let's talk about this. We can..."

I could tell from his eyes that he wasn't even hearing me. His body tensed as he prepared to launch himself at me. But before he could move, the door to Dad's office opened and a black bear launched itself into the hallway. Okay, it wasn't actually a black bear. But it *was* Mauser.

Maitland must have caught sight of Mauser's charge out of the corner of his eye because he whirled around and let out a small shriek. Mauser was delighted to meet someone new and proceeded to bounce off of Maitland before coming over to me for a quick hello. Then he circled Maitland a couple more times before deciding the new man must want to scratch him. He stopped beside him and leaned in.

Maitland was speechless. Now that Mauser's antics had come to an end, we all noticed Dad standing in the doorway. He walked over to Maitland and put out his hand. Whether Maitland was still in shock over Mauser or was just taken aback by the offered hand I don't know, but after a brief pause he took it.

"I'm deeply sorry for your loss." From the tone of Dad's voice, it was obvious this was more than a polite convention. I knew he was thinking of my mother. It had taken months for him to shake off his own depression after her sudden death, and only my suggestion that he run for sheriff—an idea she had joked with him about for years—had finally pulled him out of it.

Dad's sincerity struck a chord with Allen Maitland and his anger gave way to tears. Dad awkwardly patted him on the shoulder while Mauser leaned into him more insistently. Giving in to his grief, Maitland bent down and hugged the big dog as he cried. Finally, his emotions back under control, he stood up straight and looked Dad in the eye.

"Why did you let him go?" While he was calmer, the anger was not far below the surface.

"After we conducted a thorough investigation, I genuinely believed that he was not a suspect in the rapes," Dad answered, looking directly into Maitland's eyes.

"You were wrong," Maitland said.

"We are investigating what happened to your wife and to Jeffrey Ayers. If I was wrong, I think you can rest assured that I will no longer be sheriff." Dad's delivery was flat and emotionless, belying the pain that I knew he was feeling.

Maitland was surprised by his bluntness. "I would hope so," he said, his anger spent.

"But now we could use your help." Dad turned to me. "Is Pete in yet?"

"He should be here soon."

"Take Mr. Maitland over to the conference room and wait for him." He turned back to Maitland. "Again, I'm deeply sorry about what happened to your wife. You have my word that we won't stop looking until we've uncovered the complete truth about the circumstances surrounding her murder."

"If you'll come this way," I said, gently guiding Maitland's elbow. He hesitated for a moment, then turned and followed me to the conference room. I looked back over my shoulder to see Dad standing with his hand on Mauser's back, a mix of emotions in his eyes.

CHAPTER FOUR

I texted Pete to warn him about what he was walking into and asked him to hurry. Fifteen minutes later we were both sitting across from Maitland, conscious of the man's fresh grief, but anxious to get the interview over with.

"I want to warn you that some of the questions I have to ask might offend you," Pete started. "I'm sorry for that and there's no disrespect to your wife intended. I don't think your wife did anything wrong, but I simply have to ask specific questions. Okay?"

Maitland looked unsure, but nodded. "Whatever I can do to help figure this all out," he said softly.

"Why was your wife out at that hour of the night?"

"She's the manager at Buster's. She was in charge of closing up last night."

"What time did they close?"

"Ten. It takes her and the closing crew about an hour to clean up, count the registers and get everything ready for the morning crew. Then she goes to the bank and makes the deposit."

Her car had been found at the bank this morning. I made a note to check and see if the deposit had been made.

"Did you notice that your wife was late?"

"No." Maitland had trouble admitting this. "I get up early for my job so I don't usually wait up for her. I guess I was sleeping pretty soundly when one of your deputies knocked on our door."

"Can anyone else confirm that you were at home between eleven o'clock and midnight?"

"What the hell does that mean?"

Pete made a calming motion with his hands. "I told you, we have to ask the same questions that we would ask if this was a standard murder investigation. It doesn't mean that we suspect you of anything. We're just doing what you would want us to do, thoroughly investigate the murder of your wife."

"Yeah, I get that, but…"

"Is there anyone who can confirm you were home?"

"Maybe. We live in Spring Creek, so you know the houses are pretty close together. My truck was in our driveway. One of the neighbors may have seen it."

I doubted it. People don't really notice the normal things around their neighborhood. It's only the unusual that stands out. But maybe… We'd have to canvass the neighbors. It seemed like overkill to me, though. It was hard to imagine a scenario where Maitland killed his wife that also involved Ayers and the convenient arrival of a sheriff's deputy. Big stretch.

"Do you know Deputy Nichols?" Pete asked.

"No. But my wife did know one of the deputies. She went to school with him. He was…" Maitland choked up.

"Deputy Ortiz, yes, we know. Did you or your wife know Jeffrey Ayers?"

"No!" Anger again.

"Did you all hear about the assaults and his arrest?"

"Of course. And I had warned her to be careful. I should have done more. I just didn't think that…" His voice drifted off.

"Thank you, Mr. Maitland. We may have a few more

questions for you later, but that's all for now." Pete took out his card and turned it over, writing a number on the back and handing the card to Maitland. "That's my cell phone number on the back. Call me if you think of anything or need something."

"When will her... body... When can we bury her?"

"There has to be an autopsy, but it shouldn't be more than a day or two at most. I'll check with the coroner and get back with you as soon as possible."

We walked Maitland back to the lobby in silence and watched him walk out of the building, his shoulders hunched. As we headed back to our desks in CID, I saw Matt come out of the bathroom and walk to his desk near mine.

"Let's go back to the conference room and talk a little," I suggested to Pete.

Startled, he asked, "Why not go to our desks?"

"I don't want to be distracted by phones and co-workers," I said. What I really didn't want was for Matt to overhear us. I wasn't sure why. There was the obvious reason of Matt being friends with Chief Maxwell and me wanting this case to have as little impact on the election as possible, so the less Maxwell heard, the better. But it was more than that. Something just felt odd about this murder and the shooting. And since I was sure that Matt was working behind our backs, I just felt it would be best to keep the two separate.

I hated keeping Pete in the dark about it, but I'd promised Dad not to share our suspicions about Matt with anyone else. Luckily Pete was an easygoing guy, so if I suggested talking in the conference room he wouldn't bust my balls about it.

"It's not easy working this way," Pete said, dropping back down into a chair. I knew what he meant. Normally we went our separate ways on a case and then came back and compared notes. If we went together to interview witnesses or suspects, I usually took the lead and he listened and observed.

"Yeah, but Dad's right on this one."

"I know." Pete started to take out his cell phone, but saw the look on my face and left it in his pocket. "You want my first impression?"

"I don't know, do I?" I made the effort to joke and even managed a little smile.

"It's probably what you're looking for. Long and short, I don't like it."

"What part?"

"That's harder to say. The coincidence. Nichols finds them just after Ayers kills her? But Ayers didn't kill any of the other women he raped. If he was the rapist at all. Which I'm still not sold on. We were all part of the rape task force, or at least sat in on some of the interviews. I agreed with your father. Ayers was clear as far as I was concerned. So there's that, but there's something else too." He got quiet and stared down at the table.

"What?" I prodded.

"The clean shots."

"What?"

"Nichols comes up on a murder in progress, something he wasn't expecting. It's dark, with only his car's headlights to see by. And that light casts some very bright spots, but it also creates shadows in other places. He sees a man that he can't even be sure is a suspect... Hell, Nichols can't even be sure that a crime is in progress. Anyway, so the man turns and charges him with a knife. Now we're supposed to believe that Nichols had the presence of mind and the skill to draw his gun and fire two rounds—only two rounds—and that each of them hit their target?" He shook his head.

Pete was the department's firearms instructor. Not only was he the best shot with a rifle or pistol that we had, but he was excellent at taking a poor shooter under his wing, evaluating what they were doing wrong and helping them to correct it.

"When you put it like that, it seems unlikely."

"Under those circumstances even a great shooter would have difficulty. *You* know. Shooting a gun accurately is not as easy as people think. Even people who shoot regularly and are good at it are thrown off when they're moving, shooting at a moving target, or when it's dark. Nichols had to deal with all three. I just don't think he could do it. Trust me, he just barely meets his qualifications each year."

"So if Nichols is lying…"

"Exactly. Everything falls apart."

When Pete said that I realized just how big a mess this could be. I couldn't decide if this would make things easier or harder for Dad. Right now it looked like the whole department was coming unraveled.

"You know what you're saying?" I asked him.

"I'm accusing a fellow deputy of lying and possibly murdering a suspect. Yes, I know exactly what I'm suggesting."

"There are other questions too. If Ayers forced Angie Maitland into his car at the bank, why did he leave his car out in front of the shopping center? Why not pull around back?" I pointed out.

"Why force her into his car at all? He didn't do that with any of the other victims. He always attacked them quickly and assaulted them from behind so they couldn't see his face. And why kill her?" Pete pondered out loud.

"Maybe she saw him during the initial assault, which forced him to change his plans. He forced her into his car and realized that, having seen him, he'd have to kill her. Or maybe he planned on killing her from the beginning. Rapists sometimes turn into kidnappers or murderers."

"So did Nichols lie about how he shot him?" Pete asked.

"Maybe Nichols came upon the scene like he said, but Ayers surrendered. When Nichols saw what Ayers had done to Maitland, he went into a rage and killed Ayers in cold blood. Realizing what he did, he makes up a story of self defense," I suggested.

"I like that scenario. Not that it helps your dad. But at

least it makes Nichols's motives understandable and more in line with the deputy I know."

"I agree."

"We'll get some direction from the ballistics. Once we confirm that they're Nichols's bullets and at what distances and angles they were fired from, we'll have a better picture of what happened."

"True. Do you want to call Dr. Darzi's office?"

"You have a better relationship with him."

"But you're the lead investigator."

"Exactly, and I'm delegating the responsibility of contacting the coroner's office and prodding them into getting the autopsies done as quickly as possible to you." Game, set and match to Pete.

"Fine." I took out my cell phone. After a brief exchange with the most recent intern answering the phone, I hung up. "Dr. Darzi slept in. He's scheduled the two autopsies back to back starting at two."

"Gives us some time. We need to canvass the houses on the street alongside the store. Someone might have seen something. Also need to check the CCTV cameras around the bank and the grocery."

"I'll take the bank and any other CCTV that might have caught Ayers's or Maitland's cars."

"Don't forget Nichols's patrol car."

"Damn. Which means we need to get his dash cam footage."

"No. I checked last night when you were talking to your dad. Nichols's camera has been out for a week. He reported it when he realized it."

"A week ago?"

"Yep."

"How 'bout the dispatch recordings?"

"I called them last night and had them save the data. IT is coming in to make copies of everything."

"Okay. Meet you back here at one and we'll ride to the hospital together?"

Pete nodded and we headed our separate ways, making everything feel normal, if only for a moment.

CHAPTER FIVE

It was a mix of luck at the bank. The ATM's camera confirmed that Angie had made the deposit. A CCTV camera in the parking lot even caught footage of her car. But that was the extent of the good luck. After she'd made her deposit, the ATM video showed Angie glancing to her left as though she saw something—or someone—but then she walked off the screen to the left and there was nothing else to see.

I scanned the rest of the footage from both cameras and saw plenty of other people and cars, but there was no sign of Ayers. At one point Nichols's patrol car could be seen driving through the parking lot, but it was almost an hour before Angie Maitland made her deposit. Nothing unusual at all about a deputy on patrol cruising through a bank's parking lot at night. It's what they do.

Armed with copies of the bank videos, I drove slowly back to the office, taking the time to scope out the most direct routes between the bank and the shopping center. I took note of all the places along the routes that might have their own CCTV cameras. A lot of businesses have them these days—car lots, minute markets, fast food joints. My list had over a dozen places that would need to be checked. The trouble was, we didn't have much time to get them. A lot of places just recorded back over old footage once the tape or hard drive was full.

I called dispatch and had them patch me through to Deputy Mark Edwards. He was one of the smarter and more reliable deputies we had. I asked him to check all the locations on my list and to get copies of all footage between nine and two in the morning from the night before.

It was a long drive to the hospital in Tallahassee. You would think that a deputy would know better, but I'd had to lay down the law with Pete when we first started working together—no texting while driving. The first time he did it with me in the car, Pete tried to insist that he was just reading the messages. It got ugly, but he finally saw reason. Now he just fidgeted the whole time he was driving.

"You know, when we're in our patrol cars we're constantly reading the information that comes up on our laptops. What's the difference if I just read the occasional message?"

I glared at him. He sighed.

The hospital was quiet as we made our way down to the morgue. Dr. Darzi was already examining the body of Angie Maitland. He looked up as an intern escorted us into the large antiseptic room.

"Gentlemen," he greeted us, then continued his external inspection. I actually found this more disconcerting than the slice-and-dice part of the autopsy. It seemed very personal, looking at someone's armpits, up their nose, into their mouth and inside and around all the unmentionable parts.

"Glad you could join me this afternoon. I'll remind you that I am recording the proceedings." He tapped the microphone that hung over the table. "I keep the complete recording for the official record. So don't say anything you wouldn't want your mothers to hear." Darzi's accent had a soft Indian lilt. The man was maybe a decade older than me, but I always felt that he was in better physical and mental shape and would stay that way.

"Any thoughts yet?" Pete asked.

Darzi sighed. "I've barely started. But…" He went to the front of the table and tilted up the head. There were ugly deep purple impressions around Angie's neck. "I won't know how much damage was done until I take the X-rays and get inside, but I can tell you that she was definitely strangled with the piece of rope we found still wrapped around her neck. If it didn't cause her death, it would have. We cut it off." He pointed to an evidence bag on a counter.

"Odd. I don't remember any of the women who were assaulted mentioning that Ayers wrapped anything around their necks, or even his hands," I said.

"I think he just pushed their heads down," Pete confirmed.

"I'll be glad to compare the pictures and medical records from those assaults with my findings in this case," Darzi told us.

As Dr. Darzi conducted his examination, it soon became clear that Angie Maitland had not been raped. And there was one other odd thing. Darzi called us in close to look at the side of her head.

"Look at this laceration," he said, pointing to a spot above her left ear where a small amount of blood had matted her hair.

"I can't be sure, but from the position of the wound, and the fact that the wound bled for a while after the injury, I'd say that it happened as much as half an hour before she died."

"That's the type of injury that you could get from being shoved into a car," Pete said, having seen more than his share of them. As a deputy, you try to protect a suspect's head as you put them into the back seat of your patrol car, but if the suspect is fighting you, or if you are being intentionally rough, it's easy to leave a wound like that on the side of the person's skull.

I thought about this for a minute and tried to do the math. I took out my phone and looked at a picture I'd taken of the bank's CCTV. I'd remembered the time stamp correctly.

"If she was abducted at the bank after the deposit was made, and the murder occurred shortly before Nichols called it in, then the timeline works," I told them.

"Did you verify the time on the CCTV?" Pete asked me.

"Yes. Thanks for the confidence, big guy. I didn't fall off the turnip truck yesterday."

"The question becomes, what was he doing with her all that time, if he didn't rape her. Why did he wait to kill her?" Pete asked, ignoring my snarky response.

When Dr. Darzi switched to Ayers's body, Pete and I both moved in closer again. The gunshot wounds could tell us a lot.

Darzi pointed at the wounds as one of his assistants took pictures. "Here. See? There are traces of the heavy flannel shirt in the wound. I examined the clothing before it was removed. I didn't see any carbonaceous material or gunshot residue, which would lead me to believe that the wound was received at a distance greater than four feet... possibly more like ten. Forensics will be able to test the material.

"Now if you look here at the head wound, you'll see that there is a little bit of tattooing. I would say that this wound occurred when the victim was approximately two feet from the gun. No closer then that and, depending on the gun and type of ammunition, no more than three feet."

"So," Pete started thinking out loud, "assuming that the first round was the one in the chest, it was fired at a distance greater than four feet and the second round was fired as close as two feet from his head."

"Nothing contradicts Nichols," I said.

"You might even say that it backs him up."

Darzi was busy probing for the bullet in the brain. A new investigator might be surprised that the bullet didn't exit through the back of the head, but if you see enough gunshot wounds and follow enough bullet trails in the real world you realize that bullets do strange things. It always follows the laws of physics, but the full story often isn't obvious until you find the bullet and work backward.

Darzi brought out the bone saw and began cutting around the top of Ayers's skull. Finally, turning off the bone-jarring sound of the saw, he lifted off the skull cap. Even to my untrained eye the brain looked badly damaged.

"The bullet seems to have entered at a slight angle, causing it to curve and follow the curvature of the skull, absorbing its inertia." Darzi paused and looked up thoughtfully. "If that's the right word. I never can keep inertia and momentum straight. Doesn't matter. The result is clear. The bullet whirled around inside his skull. He would have been brain dead almost instantly." He stopped again. "Or do I mean instantaneously?" He shrugged and went back to removing what was left of the brain for sectioning.

We watched for half an hour more before we'd had enough. The forensic results would take a couple of weeks, unless something specific came up that we could press them on. Right now, nothing looked urgent.

CHAPTER SIX

"Let's stop at the crime scene," Pete said as we came into Calhoun.

I could see the orange paint on the concrete where we'd marked the positions of the bodies, Nichols's car and the rough positions where he claimed to have fired the shots.

"Okay, we've got some idea of the distance that each shot was fired from. You be Ayers," Pete said, pointing me toward the mark on the ground representing Ayers's body.

"Why do I have to be the dead guy?" I joked. "I should start back here anyway." I moved to the spot representing Angie Maitland.

"Right. I'll start roughly where the door to Nichols's car would have been."

Pete got in position, pulling out a pen to represent Nichols's gun. I got down on the ground facing the outline of Angie's body.

"Sheriff's deputy!" Pete shouted. I didn't move right away. "Stand up!" Pete ordered. "Keep your hands where I can see them."

I stood up. "We don't know if his hands were up or down," I said, turning around.

"We'll have more to go on after we formally interview

Nichols," Pete said. "But going with what we have, we know that he moved out to about here."

Pete moved to the spot where Nichols told us he was standing. This was partly verified by the nine-millimeter shell casings that we found near the spot. Ballistics would do some tests with Nichols's gun and ammunition to see where and how consistently it threw its spent casings.

When Pete stopped he was about fifteen feet away from me with his "gun" in the classic low ready position, keeping the barrel pointed safely at the ground, but ready to be raised and fired at the suspect at any sign of a threat. I charged him. Slightly surprised by the suddenness of it, Pete raised his "weapon" and attempted to get off the two shots.

"See, that doesn't work," he said. "You had your head down. My first shot wouldn't have hit you in the chest. Try again, but keep more erect."

We did it again.

"Possibly," I said, shrugging.

"Yeah. Be interesting to see what the state ballistics guys come up with when Darzi sends them the autopsy report. The actual bullet trajectories will help us map out what happened. I'll give them a nudge. They'll be willing to put a rush on it since this is a deputy-involved shooting."

"I don't think ballistics are going to solve this one."

"I'm inclined to agree with you, brother," Pete said philosophically.

The words were hardly out of his mouth when a blue Dodge pickup truck came around the corner of the store. It was moving erratically and a little too fast. Pete and I exchanged looks as the truck came to an abrupt stop about fifty feet in front of us. A middle-aged man jumped out of the cab and headed toward us, weaving ever so slightly. He had oily, uncut hair, an untrimmed beard and was wearing boots, jeans and a dirty flannel shirt.

"Who are you two?" he demanded, his eyes burning.

"Deputies Macklin and Henley," I said, pulling my coat back far enough so that the star on my belt showed. There are times when you have to bow up and put on your *I'm in charge, you're not* attitude, and it's almost always called for when you're dealing with someone who's had a bit too much to drink.

In this case all I did was set him off. He lunged clumsily and half swung a fist at me. "You sonsofbitches," he managed to both yell and mumble at the same time, which was quite a feat.

I grabbed his arm and pulled it behind his back, causing him to fall to his knees.

"Letgoofme!" he yelled. "Youbastards! Youkilledmy brotheryouassholes." He screamed incoherently then started to cry. The tension went out of him and he became dead weight. I let go of his arm and he slumped the rest of the way to the ground.

"Mr. Ayers, we're out here trying to figure out what happened last night," I told him. "If your brother was treated unfairly, we're as interested in finding that out as you are."

He had his head buried in his arms as he cried. Finally, he wiped his eyes and rolled over. I suspect that with the alcohol and the grief, he couldn't have stood up if he'd wanted to.

"My brother never did nothin' to no women," he slurred. "But you killed him anyway."

"How do you know he didn't assault those women?" Pete asked, standing over him.

"Don't think he could," the man said. "You don't understand. He was nice. I was the asshole." He said this last slowly and deliberately.

"Come on, sit up." I offered him my hand. He took it and I pulled him upright. He flipped over onto his knees and finally staggered to his feet. I helped him over to Pete's car, where he leaned heavily against the hood.

"What's your name?"

"I'm Wayne. I'm Wayne Ayers and my brother is Jeffrey Ayers. Damn you," he said sadly.

"Wayne, you seem sure that your brother couldn't have assaulted those women. Was he... gay?" I asked.

His eyes got wide for a moment and I worried that he might come off the car swinging at me again. But he just put his head back and laughed. "Jeffrey gay? No, lord, no. Don't make me laugh." He stopped laughing and his eyes seemed to sober up. "Look, talk to his girlfriend. Candace Lansky..."

He seemed to lose his train of thought to the alcohol for a moment, but managed to get back on track. "Lives over on the north side. Go talk to her. She'll set you straight." He looked sick and leaned back across the hood of Pete's car.

"Look, we can't let you drive home. I'm going to park your truck in the lot, lock it up and we'll drop you off at your mom's." Pete didn't wait for a response as he walked over to the truck and drove it around to the front of the shopping center. I stayed with the sad and drunk Wayne Ayers. When Pete came back we were at least able to return one son home safe to his mother.

It was after six by the time Pete dropped me off at my car. "I'm headed home," I told Cara, calling her as soon as I was moving in the right direction.

"Long day?" She sounded tired herself.

"A bit. Yours?"

"Tough."

"Dinner?"

"Let me feed Alvin and give him a bit of attention, then I'll be over." Alvin was the Pug she'd rescued when he was abandoned at the vet.

"Deal."

"I've got some sauce. Do you have some spaghetti?"

"Actually, I do. Surprised?"

"You always surprise me."

I hung up with a smile on my face. We'd only been seriously dating for a month, but I'd never felt this comfortable with a woman. Maybe not with anyone. It was amazing how stupid banter about dinner arrangements could make me feel so good.

The winter sun was long gone by the time I drove down the dirt road that led to my doublewide on twenty acres. It was easy to feel like I was leaving the job behind when I came home. I could see the soft glow of town in the distance, but here the moonlight dominated the sky. Tonight the moon was full and it cast enough blue-tinged light that I could walk under the live oaks to my house without stumbling.

Ivy met me at the door, rubbing against my legs until I fed her dinner. I took a hot shower and changed, then hurried to put water on for the spaghetti. I was still trying to impress Cara with all the life skills I'd mastered.

"And I *am* impressed," she said as she heated up her homemade sauce.

"I can even make garlic bread!"

"Okay, don't overdo it. You'll just set yourself up for failure," she joked, smiling as I spread butter on the bread, sprinkled it with garlic salt and slid the tray into the oven with a flourish.

After she turned back to stir the sauce, I spent a moment savoring the sight of her. The red hair and Irish complexion she got from her mother went well with the strong jaw that came from her Nordic father. Whenever I looked at her I always felt like I could see the joy inside of her. If it wasn't actually displayed in her eyes and her laughter, I could sense it just below the surface, waiting to return with a smile.

"That's done enough," she proclaimed. "Let's eat."

After we'd taken the edge off our hunger, I said, "You sounded like your day was pretty rough." I gave her an opening without pushing. We still weren't familiar enough with each other for me to tell if she wanted to talk about her bad day or leave it behind.

"It was pretty awful. We lost a dog. A Bassett. He was old, but such a sweetie." I could hear her choke up.

"You don't have to talk about it."

"I know, but it's all right. We helped him over the Rainbow Bridge." She paused and looked at me. "I guess that sounds corny."

"No, not at all," I said sincerely. "My faith is not always as secure it should be, but I've never doubted that a good dog goes to heaven. A good cat too!" I said to Ivy, who was watching us from the couch.

"Of course, the things I see at the vet are nothing compared to what you have to deal with most days. I guess that's why you've thought you'd rather do something else with your life."

"It is. But I've watched my dad, and he seems to have done a pretty good job of balancing things. If he can, then so can I."

"He seems like a good man." Cara had known my dad in passing from his visits to the vet with Mauser, but he'd insisted on a formal introduction at Christmas. I was encouraged that she hadn't been scared off by him.

"He has his moments. But Dad can be the proverbial bull in the china shop sometimes." I loved my father, but there was a lot of truth in that statement.

"How bad is all of this going to be for him?"

"I don't know. A lot depends on what Pete and I can find out."

"How's that going?"

"I hate having to follow Pete around but, understandably, Dad doesn't want me out on point with this one. But we've decided we can split up a bit. In fact, I'm going out in the morning to interview a woman who knew Ayers."

"Was he the rapist?"

"When we turned him loose, we didn't think so." I shrugged. "But who knows? We all make mistakes. Unfortunately, in law enforcement, if you make a bad enough mistake people can get hurt."

Cara raised her hands. "Sorry, that's enough talking about sad things." We got up and cleared the table, which included clearing Ivy, who had come over to lick the plates clean.

We spent the rest of the evening watching a silly movie, cuddled together under a blanket as the heat was barely able to keep up with the dropping temperatures outside. Cara was opening the vet's office the next morning, so she couldn't stay the night, but for a few hours at least, all was right with the world.

CHAPTER SEVEN

The next morning, I took my time getting up and out. There was no hurry since I wanted to talk with Candace Lansky before going to the office. For a casual interview I'd found it best to give people a chance to get beyond their morning routines before I started asking questions.

Once on the road, I called dispatch and asked them to check the DMV records for her address. She lived in a small house on the north side. It wasn't one of the better areas of the county, but the road she lived on wasn't the worse. I looked at my watch—almost nine. I was running the risk of missing her if she had a job to get to, but I'd take my chances.

There was a car in the driveway so I seemed to be in luck. I knocked on the door several times before it opened. No worries about her rushing off to work. She stood there staring at me, wearing a robe and a snarky expression. She obviously needed quite a while for *her* morning routine.

"Who the hell are you?" Candace Lansky asked.

"Sorry to bother you. I'm Deputy Larry Macklin. I'm investigating the death of Jeffrey Ayers."

She looked me dead in the eye and said, "It's not enough that you shot him dead, you have to go around and wake up all his friends? I heard you were harassing Wayne yesterday."

"That's not exactly what happened."

She held up her hand to stop me. "Wayne is the victim in every story he tells. S'okay, come in. I'm freezing my tits off."

She stepped back, holding the door open. All the blinds were drawn, making the living room dark and gloomy. The room smelled of stale cigarettes and liquor. "Have a seat." She waved toward a saggy couch.

"You were friends with Jeffrey Ayers?"

She took a pack of cigarettes out of her pocket and lit one. "Yeah, that's right."

"More than friends?"

"Yeah, more than friends. We were going steady." Candace said the last bit with irony and a hearty laugh. She probably wasn't any older than me, but life had already ridden her hard.

"Wayne said that you could tell me why Jeffrey couldn't have been the rapist."

"Wayne talks too much." I thought that was all she was going to say, but then she went on. "My fault for pouring my heart out to that blabber-mouth. If any of you had asked me, I'd have sworn on a stack of Bibles that Jeffrey Ayers couldn't rape no woman." She suddenly seemed to be enjoying the dramatic effect of the moment. I realized that she was going to make me ask.

"Okay, I'll bite. Why couldn't he have raped those women? Was he impotent?" Not that that would prove anything. Some rapists were impotent with their girlfriends or wives, but they were perfectly capable when they attacked other women.

Candace got up. "Follow me."

I got up and followed her warily through a dark hallway. When we came to a door, she stopped and seemed to think for a moment before flinging it open. Inside was a large king size bed with ropes and handcuffs strapped to all four posts. Various whips, ropes and chains hung on the walls throughout the room. I looked from the room to Candace.

"It's my thing." She shrugged.

I can't say I was that shocked. During the time I was on patrol, I went into a lot of people's houses and saw a lot of strange things. Once we had to rescue a guy who'd dressed himself head to toe in a rubber suit and then couldn't get out of his bathtub.

"And what exactly does this have to do with Jeffrey Ayers?"

She sighed heavily and headed back toward the living room. When we were seated again she explained, "He was my boyfriend for five years. I wanted him to tie me up, whip me, even choke me. Nothin'. The few times that we tried it, he couldn't get hard. He was just a nice guy, a really nice guy.

"I got so frustrated toward the end of our relationship that I tried to piss him off. It worked a couple times. Once he even grabbed me. When he did that… Well, it didn't excite him, if you know what I mean. In fact, he had a panic attack and it took me the rest of the evening to calm him down." She sighed again, as though just the memory of it exhausted her.

"Having it offered to you isn't necessarily the same as stalking someone and assaulting them."

"You don't get it… Or you don't want to get it. The guy could screw. He liked it, but only if we talked sweet and hugged. At his house… Did you look in his room?"

We'd searched his room when he was brought in for questioning. I'd actually helped go through his stuff. "Yes," I said, not knowing where she was going with this.

"Did you find anything unusual?" she asked, eyebrows lifted.

I thought back. I remembered that his room was cluttered. "I know there weren't any whips or chains."

"Damn right. You didn't find anything you thought odd to be in a grown man's room?"

"There were some kid's toys," I remembered.

"Big stuffed giraffe? A tiger?"

"I remember the tiger. So?"

"He slept with those. Any odd books?"

"There were a lot of romances. I assumed they were his mother's."

"You assumed wrong. The man was sweet. Really too sweet for my taste. When I first saw all that, I thought he was a fruit or something. But no, just a soft, cuddly oaf. Any woman who knew him would never, ever believe he could sexually attack someone. You all screwed the pooch with that one."

I thought about that. We went in looking for evidence to support our belief that he was involved in the attacks and skipped over all the odd stuff. And it made sense that he wouldn't have used his own tenderness as a defense. He'd probably spent most of his life hiding it from other guys. What guy wants to admit that he sleeps with stuffed animals and reads romance novels? And would we have believed him anyway?

"But we did release him. We realized he didn't do it," I said in our defense.

"But now one of your deputies shot him 'cause he thought he'd attacked another woman. I don't know much, but I know that Jeffrey Ayers didn't attack that woman, sexually or otherwise."

We looked at each other for a moment. *I believe her, and that changes everything*, I thought.

"You can shut the door on your way out," Candace said, lighting another cigarette from the stub of the one she took out of her mouth.

When I checked my phone there was a text from Dad asking me to come by his house at lunch. I was well aware that it said "at lunch" and not "for lunch." Dad had a basic philosophy that it was every man for himself when it came to food and drink.

Pete was going over reports from the night before. Even

though we were working on the double shooting, we still had other cases to follow up on. Since the shooting was high priority and was going to involve a lot of our time, we needed to clear the others out of the way. Lt. Johnson had agreed to take us off of the on-call rotation, while letting us know that we'd be doing double duty in the future to make up for it.

"I'll have these finished up in no time. Luckily, Matt picked up that drug-related homicide a couple of weeks ago. I wouldn't want to have to be dealing with that right now."

Hearing Matt's name reminded me of our other grim outstanding issue. I wondered if that's what Dad wanted to meet with me about.

"By the way, how'd your meeting with Candace go?" Pete asked. I took him to the conference room and filled him in.

"Damn," he sighed.

"Now you know why I wanted us to talk in here."

"Yeah, there are enough media vultures interested in picking the corpses clean. Not that I think someone in our office would give them the information."

"Of course not. They'd be sure to sell or trade it," I said, only half joking.

"Sad state of affairs." Pete shook his head dramatically. "I had Edwards go door to door last night when he had some downtime, checking the houses close to the shopping center to see if anybody heard or saw anything."

"And…?"

"A couple people think they heard the shots, but aren't sure."

"Sounds very helpful," I said sarcastically. Eye- and ear-witnesses are only useful in a small percentage of cases. That doesn't mean that prosecutors and defense attorneys don't use them in most cases. They use them for the very reason that they *aren't* usually reliable. Witnesses can be suggestible and they often have their own agendas. A lot of the time they just want to be helpful, but that in itself is problematic. When you're investigating a crime, you don't want a witness to tell you what they *think* you want to hear, but often that's just what they do.

"We should check them out anyway," Pete said. He loved talking to people, which was one of the reasons he was as good an investigator as he was.

Then Pete got real quiet.

"I know what you're thinking," I said. "We've got a mess. I'm convinced that Ayers didn't assault those women. So the question now is, did he kill Angie Maitland? Maybe. But why was he lying on top of her, if he wasn't capable of rape? And why didn't he just drive her behind the store after abducting her from the bank?"

"And how did a deputy who is a crap shot manage to get off two shots on a moving target under stress? I checked his gun and magazine and those were the only two rounds fired." I could hear the frustration in Pete's voice

"And if Nichols is lying, why? And about how much? Maybe he came up on Angie and Jeffrey while they were having some sort of affair, recognized Ayers, thought that he was assaulting her and killed him."

"And then killed Angie? That seems a little far-fetched. Why didn't she have more bruises or show signs of a struggle?" Pete wondered.

"Nichols holds the gun on her and has her wrap the rope around her neck. Then he strangles her with it."

"Maybe." Pete didn't sound convinced. "We need to interview Nichols. I think he's had enough time to get himself together. I'll call him and ask him to come in this afternoon."

"Just let me know when. I've got to go meet Dad for lunch," I said, getting up from the table.

CHAPTER EIGHT

When I pulled up to his house, I could see Dad walking out to the barn. He looked up and gave me a small wave. As I followed Dad to the barn, Mauser came bounding from the back of the house and almost knocked me down with his ridiculously enthusiastic winter greeting. If it had been summer, I'd have only received a couple of barks from the shade of the house.

"We eating hay?"

"What?" Dad asked distractedly as he got a halter off the rack and an alfalfa cube from a bucket of treats by the door.

"You invited me to lunch," I pointed out.

"Working lunch, without the food," he said soberly. It was clear that he wasn't going to be kidded into a good mood. He went to the gate that separated the barn from the turnout and called for Finn and Mac.

"Grab Mac's halter," he told me.

"I'm wearing my good clothes," I pointed out.

"You've got some old ones in the house. Go change and I'll help get Mac ready for you."

I looked around, trying to come up with an excuse, but nothing came to mind. *Better just relax and go with it*, I thought. The weather was beautiful for January, a brisk sixty degrees and a clear blue sky from one horizon to the next. There were worse ways to spend the next hour.

"I'll be back in a minute," I said as Finn and Mac, a pair of seven year-old bays, came cantering up to the gate.

By the time I'd changed into jeans, a thermal shirt and a corduroy jacket and made it back to the barn, Dad had both the horses brushed and Finn was saddled. I finished up with Mac and we led them outside.

The horses, a rare set of twins out of champion old-stock American Quarter Horses, had been given to Dad by a grateful friend. Dad had tracked down and recovered the man's stolen horse trailer and a large amount of tack. They were named after the mythical Irish folk hero Fionn mac Cumhaill and had very different personalities. Finn was curious, courageous to the point of recklessness and was constantly restless under saddle, ready to break into a canter at the first request. Mac, on the other hand, lived for mealtimes, was always happy to be twenty paces behind his brother and took a nap at every opportunity.

"Wanted a little saddle time before the parade." Dad answered my unasked question, referring to the upcoming Great Americans parade in Calhoun. I also knew that riding took him away from his troubles. My grandfather had had a mean streak when he was drunk and Dad learned early that a horse was a great way to put some distance between himself and an ugly situation.

We headed out on a trail that went around the pasture and into an area of longleaf pines and palmettos. I trotted Mac a little to catch up to Dad and Finn.

"You all find out anything?" he asked when I finally came abreast.

"Just that Ayers didn't rape those women," I said, relishing the reaction I'd get. I wasn't disappointed. Dad's head whipped around and he looked me square in the eye, trying to tell if I was making a joke.

"How can you be sure?" he asked, trying not to sound too hopeful.

"What I've found out isn't evidence, but it's pretty solid. Ayers was a big baby. His ex-girlfriend said that he couldn't even pretend to be aggressive and get it up."

"Could she be protecting him?"

"Didn't come across that way at all. I think we can find other people who'd back her up."

"But it's anecdotal."

"Afraid so. Funny how that can be more convincing than hard evidence sometimes," I said, as much to myself as to Dad.

"True. People have core values, and it takes a lot for them to go against their own nature." He paused. "Knowing he wasn't the rapist makes me feel better. But it creates a whole 'nother set of problems."

"Exactly. Pete and I have raised the question of who the rapist was back up to the top of the list, just below who killed Angie Maitland. And, of course, those may or may not be the same person."

"You and Pete can have all the resources and time you need. I'll tell Lt. Johnson not to give you all any other cases for a couple of weeks. I can always move someone off of patrol to handle some of the burglaries and auto thefts."

"We're on it," I said sincerely.

"I know that and I appreciate it." He was quiet for a couple of minutes. I encouraged Mac to keep up. I could tell there was something else on Dad's mind.

"I checked over the report on Matt's movements," he finally said, not looking at me. "It doesn't look good. He's up to something... I'm going to open Finn up a little."

That was said as a warning. As soon as Dad gave Finn his head and put a little bit of leg on him, the horse launched into a canter. I pushed Mac into a faster trot and finally a reluctant canter, trying to at least keep Finn and Dad in sight.

We wound our way through the pine trees and palmettos. Mac was sweating and blowing by the time Dad reined Finn in. Honestly, I was panting a little too. Riding is more work than most people realize.

55

"I thought I'd better put him through his paces a little before the parade. You're going to be riding in it this year."

"That sounds like an order," I joked.

"It is," he deadpanned. "This is an election year. I'm putting pressure on all of the posse to be there."

The Adams County Sheriff's Mounted Posse was one quarter ceremonial and three quarters practical. Made up of volunteers with their own horses, the posse was vital for searching for missing persons or for hunting evidence in terrain where cars or even four-wheelers couldn't go.

"Bob's got them looking pretty good," Dad said. Bob Muller was a retired deputy with a love of horses and law enforcement who'd volunteered to be the posse's coordinator.

"I'll be there. At least it's only the one parade."

Five years ago there had been two parades within a month—one for Martin Luther King Jr. Day and the other for Presidents' Day. The county sheriff, the city police, the fire department and all the rest of the city and county departments had had to participate in both parades. The cost and time drove both governments crazy, but politically they had no choice. The two parades were basically segregated, with both sides of the civilian population refusing to celebrate with the other. Finally the Presbyterian minister and the good reverend from Bethel First Christian Church got together and came up with a plan to consolidate the parades. Their proposal called for a Great Americans parade that would fall between MLK Day and Presidents' Day. The city council and the county commission gaveled the motion through so fast that it was a done deal before anyone had a chance to nitpick it to death. Honestly, I considered it one of our local governments' proudest moments.

We reached the far end of the trail and began to circle back. Mac knew we were headed home and was now more than willing to keep up with Finn.

"What are you going to do about Matt?" I finally asked.

"He's been hanging out in some seedy parts of the

county. One place he's been spending time is about half a block from the Sweet Spot," Dad said through tight lips.

I knew that betrayal was the one thing that could drive him to violence. I'd once watched him break his fist slamming it into a wall. The wall had been a stand-in for a captain who'd disobeyed an order and purposely sent his men into a situation that could have gotten them killed.

"I'll call Eddie and see if he has any new information." Eddie was my one and only confidential informant.

"Do you really think he's trustworthy?" Dad asked.

"I do."

"But he's a Thompson," he said, referring to one of the largest and more notorious families in the county. They weren't all bad, but they were all strange, and more than a few of them were involved in the local drug trade.

"I told you, he has personal reasons as well as financial ones for helping me."

Eddie, the grandson of the Thompson patriarch, was also a cross-dresser who had been emotionally and physically abused by his family. He'd know all about the Sweet Spot. It was a dive bar that, on any Saturday night, saw more drug sales than the Walgreens did in a month. Most of the drugs were distributed by a black gang, but the drugs were imported, cut and managed by members and associates of the Thompson clan. This had been on Dad's radar for a few years now, but he'd never been able to get enough evidence on them to make the charges stick.

"I'm not sure you and I can handle the situation with Matt," Dad said, sounding pessimistic.

"You could let a few more of our people in on this."

"Not yet. I want some clear evidence before I reveal this pile of crap."

I trusted Dad's instincts. He had been a good deputy and a great investigator because he knew when to bring the curtain down on any given situation. That's one of the hardest calls to make as a law enforcement officer. Bust the door down too soon and you won't catch all the bad guys;

do it too late and a firestorm erupts and people get hurt.

"Talk to your informant and let me know if he has anything. One way or another, we need to get in closer and get a clear picture of what Matt is doing," he said through more gritted teeth.

Mauser greeted us as we came back to the barn, his big brown eyes asking if it was lunch time yet.

"You ate breakfast and went back to bed, and I know you didn't move while we were gone. How the hell can you be that hungry?" Dad asked him. Mauser went over to the shade and fell over, pretending to die of starvation. Finally I saw Dad smile.

CHAPTER NINE

A text from Pete let me know that Isaac Nichols was coming in at three for a formal interview. I decided that I had enough time to check out one or two of the witnesses that Deputy Edwards had talked to. I called dispatch and asked them to have Edwards meet me in the shopping center parking lot.

A few minutes later he pulled up to my car, driver's side to driver's side in the classic cops-bullshitting-with-each-other formation.

"I found two people who thought they'd heard something that night," Edwards said, giving me their addresses. He was short and dark haired. He looked more like an English teacher than a deputy, and he wrote his reports more like a novelist than a cop.

"I wouldn't bother with the first one. The guy was coming home from his job in Tallahassee and thought he might or might not have heard something. Now the other one was your classic Agatha Christie, nosy old lady type. You might know her. Maggie Gavin. She made it a big point to tell me that she was the founder of the local neighborhood watch."

The name sounded familiar. "What'd she say?"

"She was being pretty cagey, trying to leverage the information for some face-to-face time with someone higher up the food chain than me."

"You're kidding!"

"She's a piece of work. I had to deal with her last year when some kids were busting up mailboxes. Phone calls at two in the morning. I kid you not. She hears all and knows all. Go by, tell her you're an investigator and the sheriff's son, and you'll probably get an earful. But I wouldn't doubt she makes stuff up, so take it all with a big grain of salt."

"I can't wait," I said, then added, "Did you get a chance to pull any of that CCTV footage yet?"

"Yeah, I left the copies on your desk. I looked through them and didn't see much."

I thanked him then steeled myself for the meeting with our local Miss Marple.

I pulled up to a small block house painted a garish blue with white shutters. The yard was well kept and the flowerbeds neatly trimmed, ready for warmer weather. The neighborhood was made up of what would have been called working-class homes thirty years earlier. They were close together, and while some of the small yards had toys scattered about, others were full of the kitschy lawn stuff that old folks always seem to like.

The door opened almost before I could get out of the car. A stooped woman with lasers for eyes stepped out onto the small concrete front porch.

"You with the police," she said, more as a statement than a question.

"I'm an investigator with the sheriff's office," I told her. I started to show her my star, but she waved it away.

"I know a cop when I see one. And that car practically screams law enforcement. Hope you don't expect to fool anyone with that," she said sternly, waving a hand at my unmarked vehicle. Finally, after giving me the eye from head to foot, she turned and went into the house. "Come on, you're letting all my heat out. Wipe your feet good."

I followed her into a very neat and uncluttered living room. I'd expected it to be full of knickknacks, but it was almost Spartan in its decor. The furniture dated back to the seventies, but looked brand new with plastic covers over all the cushions. This was not a crazy cat lady.

"I'm Deputy Larry Macklin," I said once we were seated.

"Macklin? Like the sheriff?"

"I'm his son." For the first time, she looked at me with interest rather than like a freak insect that had wandered into her yard.

"Good. I've got a few things I need your father to take care of. Our neighborhood has some troublemakers and idiots. You know that I founded the neighborhood watch?"

"Deputy Edwards did mention that," I said, tugging at my collar. She must have had the heat turned up to eighty degrees. I was already sweating. "He also said that you heard something the other night."

"The night of the murder? Yes, I did. First, let me give you my list."

She got up surprisingly fast for a person of her age. Before I had a chance to stop her, she'd headed to the back of the house. A minute later she came out carrying four pages of notes, single-spaced, and handed them to me. They were detailed lists of various infractions of the law and suspicious activities that had occurred over the last couple of weeks.

"Normally, I email those. But lately I haven't been getting a reply. I suspect that my reports aren't getting to the sheriff. Here, I'll go over them with you."

"Really, this is great," I said, holding up the report. "I can go over them with the sheriff later. Right now I…"

Her eyes went cold. The last person who'd looked at me that way had broken a bottle he was holding and lunged at me with it.

"I want to go over this first so I know that you know

61

what problems we're having here in the neighborhood." Her voice was flat.

I smiled broadly, giving in. "Of course. You're right."

We spent the next half hour poring over the report, where she had highlighted every time that a neighbor did anything that she considered to be out of line.

"Assure me that you will go over this with your father. I'm especially interested in having him take a personal interest in the Goodsons. They don't seem to be able to understand the trouble that can follow if they let their trashcans overflow like they do. The broken window syndrome. Once a neighborhood looks neglected, the hoodlums move in."

"Absolutely," I agreed.

"I went down to Orlando for the neighborhood crime prevention conference a couple years ago."

"We really appreciate your efforts. Now, about the murder…"

"I guess I've raked you over the coals enough," she said with a gleam in her eye. "Come over here."

She got up and I followed her into the kitchen. She pointed through the window over the sink, which was completely lacking the frilly curtains or potted plants that you'd expect in an old woman's home. In fact, there was only a set of plain blinds that she had drawn up as high as they would go.

"There, you see? I can look right out to the back of the store."

She was right. There was a large pecan tree in her backyard, but this time of year it didn't have any leaves on it. The back of the shopping center was about two hundred yards away. If you moved to the far left side of her sink, you could see the dumpster.

"What did you see that night?"

"I came to the sink for a glass of water and I looked out." I didn't bother to stop her and ask if it was normal for her to look out the window. We'd clearly established that she was a busybody. "I saw a light over there, behind the store."

"What kind of light?"

"At first it was the headlights of a car. It stopped, which made me suspicious. We've had trouble with folks coming behind the store late at night in their cars and doing... Well, God knows what. I've had to call the sheriff's office at least every other month."

"Did you call on Wednesday night?" I asked and got a squinty-eyed glare from her.

"The people doing you all's dispatch can be mighty rude sometimes. I've learned to wait until I've got something firm to report. Wednesday I thought I'd watch for a few minutes and see if the car stayed there or moved on. If your 911 people appreciated me more, I might have called and stopped a murder." She said the last in an accusatory tone, not approving of the 911 operator's efforts to cut down on crank calls.

"So you saw the headlights of a car behind the store..."

"That's right. After a minute or two, the lights went out. At least the headlights went out. I could still see the parking lights. Maybe even some glow from the... What do you call them... fog lights."

"But you couldn't see the car?" It would have been impossible with the naked eye, but for all I knew she had a professional-grade pair of binoculars under the sink.

"No."

"What happened next?"

"Well, to say the least, that got my attention. So I kept watching. Thought they might be breaking into the store or something. Of course, more likely they were doing some dirty business." She shook her head. "After a couple of minutes, I saw the headlights come on again and then there were a couple gunshots. I could even see the flashes. It was a little odd because I saw the flashes before I heard the sound."

"Did you see the deputy's car pull up?"

"I told you, it was already there. He turned his police

lights on, and then I heard and saw the shots." Mrs. Gavin looked at me like I was stupid. I *was* feeling a little stupid right at that moment.

"So you're saying that the car you saw pull up and turn its headlights off was the patrol car?" I was trying to come to terms with what this might mean.

"That's right. I'm sure of it."

"Could you see anything else before the rest of the first responders showed up?"

"No, not really. It was only a few minutes. Maybe five before the next patrol car showed up."

"Thank you, Mrs. Gavin." I pulled out one of my cards. "If any other officer comes by to ask you questions, call me first. Don't even let them in before you've talked to me. Understand?"

She heard the tone of my voice and saw the look on my face and for the first time since I'd arrived, she looked uncertain.

"Yes. Okay, if you think that's best. But why...?"

I held up my hand and stopped her. "You are now very important to this investigation. I think that you could earn the personal gratitude of the sheriff if you follow my directions to the letter." The only way I could think to get this woman to take it seriously and do as I said was to appeal to her pride.

"Yes, of course." It worked. Now she sounded like a member of the French Resistance assuring her comrades that she could be trusted.

After another warning or two, I was back in my car headed to the office. Things had taken a very black turn for Deputy Nichols. Nichols, Matt... Could we really have that many dirty cops? Eddie, my CI, had suggested that there could be more than one. But I was never sure when he was being straight and when he was being overly dramatic.

CHAPTER TEN

I had about ten minutes with Pete before Nichols was scheduled to arrive. I brought him up to speed on my interview with Mrs. Gavin, and we agreed not to confront Nichols with what we now knew.

"We'll just get his side of the story for the record," Pete said.

"Let him dig a hole that we can bury him in later," I agreed.

"I explained to Major Parks that we had some questions about Nichols's account. Parks said that he'd let us take the lead for now, and just to keep him up to date." Then Pete shook his head. "This is some crazy shit. Something very wrong went on behind that store. Finding out what and why isn't going to be easy."

"Especially with two of the three witnesses dead," I mumbled to myself.

We'd been talking in the conference room, which had a door with a small vertical window. Through the window I saw Deputy Nichols as he walked past, headed into CID.

"There he is," I said, taking a deep breath to steady my nerves. Nothing is harder for me than hiding revulsion from a suspect.

Pete went out to bring him back to the conference room. We'd decided not to use one of the more official interview rooms in order to put Nichols more at ease... And the better to encourage him to run his mouth. Most criminals sink their boat by filling it up with their own words.

I smiled when they came in and shook Nichols's hand while Pete invited him to have a seat.

"Thanks, guys. I wanted to get this interview over with today so it isn't hanging over me all weekend. I really need to get back to work. The wife is killing me with her honey-do list."

Pete and I smiled and chuckled politely at his predicament.

"We want to get you back on the street too. The other deputies are tired of picking up your slack," Pete joked. "Okay. Are you sure that you don't want anyone else present?" We all knew that he was talking about a lawyer.

"No. I'm fine." Nichols looked relaxed.

"Of course we'll be recording this." Pete took a small recorder out of his pocket and set it on the table. Nichols nodded his head. It was standard procedure to record this sort of interview.

"Let's start with your last call." I knew that Pete wanted to begin with verifiable facts, and then move forward into whatever story Nichols was going to tell.

Nichols pulled out his phone. "I've got my notes here." All deputies are encouraged to keep and retain notes. Having something to refer to when you're being questioned by attorneys can save you some heartache.

"At eleven-fifteen I responded to a domestic dispute. When I got to 1754 West Carver Street, the wife told me that she and her husband had been fighting, but it was over. I took her outside to my car where she could talk without the chance of her husband hearing. She assured me that there was no problem and that there would not be any more trouble. I left the call at eleven-forty." Nichols looked up from his notes. All of that had been verified by the dispatch records.

"You left the domestic call... What then?" Pete asked, nonchalantly making notes on his pad.

"Things were quiet, so I decided to cruise some of my regular spots."

"Regular spots?"

"You know, places where I knew something might be going down. I went by the Fast Mart on Jefferson. There's always some lowlifes hanging out there. Some of the regulars were there and I checked in with them, but nothing was up that night. After that, I decided to drive over to the shopping center and see if anyone was parked out back."

"Okay, go slow now and tell us everything you did from the moment you pulled into the parking lot," Pete said, looking a little more interested while trying not to seem too aggressive.

"Sure. I pulled into the drive off of Jefferson and proceeded around the north side of the building."

"Okay. I know when I'm checking out a spot, I sometimes try and sneak up. You know, turn my radio down, maybe my lights off. You do anything like that?"

For a moment I thought Pete had gone too far. Nichols looked at him with a funny expression, but went on. "No. I just drove around the back."

"When did you first see Ayers and the woman?"

"I saw his legs when I got about halfway down the backside of the building. I thought it might be a homeless guy sleeping by the dumpster. But as I got closer and turned my car toward them, I could see that he was trying to have sex with someone."

I had to bite back the urge to put some pressure on him now. We knew he was lying, but Nichols was too savvy to fall for our usual interview techniques.

"So you stopped?" I asked.

"Right. I pulled in and stopped where you found my car. I still thought they were probably having consensual sex. I've found prostitutes in front of the store in the past who take johns behind it to do the dirty."

Why did he emphasize that he parked his car and didn't move it? I wondered. "You got out of the car then?"

"Right. I got out, pulled out my flashlight and pointed it at them."

"But you didn't call it in?"

"No. I... Well, I thought it might be someone that I could just let off with a warning. Like I said, I was still pretty sure it was consensual." He acted embarrassed that he might have let people off who were breaking the law. It's a ploy of the guilty to pretend to have committed a minor offense and feel bad about it in order to gain sympathy from the interviewer. It also implies that you are baring your soul when, in reality, you're hiding a crime.

"You're out of the car. You've got your flashlight in your hand..." Pete encouraged Nichols.

"Yes, that's right. I put my other hand... my right hand, back on my gun. Looking at them, I got a weird vibe right off. The guy seemed to be just lying on top of the woman. I told them that I was a deputy and that they needed to get up."

"What exactly did you say?"

"Think it was: 'Sheriff's deputy! Stand up slowly.' But still there wasn't any response. From either of them. Alarm bells were really going off now. You know what I mean?" Nichols asked us. Another ploy to get us on his side? Pete just nodded.

"So I put my flashlight back in its holster and drew my gun. I switched on the light when I did." The officers on night patrol all had small flashlights fixed to the tops of their Glock handguns. "This time I yelled at them, ordering them to stand up and turn around slowly, hands in sight."

Nichols stopped talking and seemed to be lost in a world of his own mind's creation. "Go on," I encouraged, trying not to sound too cynical.

"That's when Ayers spoke. He said: 'Officer, we're just having a little fun.' And he started to get up. I kept my gun on him. The girl was motionless. Of course I know now that she was dead, but I think it was partly the way her body looked... lifeless... that had me wired. Usually, you come upon a couple having sex and the girl's all squirming and upset. This was the first time one ever just laid there."

"Let's go slow from here. As much detail as you can remember," Pete prompted.

"Yeah, I admit that some of it is kind of fuzzy. I think I reacted as much by instinct as anything else."

"That's understandable. Just do the best you can."

"I had my gun up in a ready position. Ayers started to get up and I thought there was something in his hand so I yelled: 'Keep your hands where I can see them!' He said something... I don't remember what. I don't even think I really heard it. Just something in a real soothing tone. But my eyes were focused on his hands like they train us. Funny, I can still hear you saying that." This last was to Pete.

"Might have saved your life."

"I think it did. There was just a second when I saw the knife clearly as he turned and charged me. At that point, my training took over. I pulled the trigger twice without being conscious of doing it." Nichols was pretty much ignoring Pete's request for details. If he was lying, as I was pretty sure he was, he was smart enough to know that the details would be hard to keep consistent if he had to repeat his story during multiple interviews.

We went over the aftermath of the shooting pretty quickly. Nichols wasted no time bringing the story up to the time when everything was verifiable by multiple witnesses. Pete didn't ask for anything more. We'd agreed that one of the goals of the interview was to have Nichols walk out of it still thinking that we believed everything he was telling us. We shook his hand, made a little more small talk and sent him on his way.

"What do you think?" Pete asked, sitting his bulk back down in a chair.

"He's lying through his teeth," I said.

"Probably. But we have to prove it. And, honestly, there's still a small chance that the shooting was justified, but that he's lying about some of the details. But that wouldn't fundamentally put him in the evil perp category."

I gave Pete a skeptical look.

"What I'm saying is, he might not be a cold-blooded killer, that's all." Pete took his cell phone out of his pocket and checked for messages. Even the possibility of Nichols being a murderer couldn't overcome his addiction to texting his wife and daughters.

"I think you're leaning over backward to be fair."

"Well, he's not going anywhere, and Major Parks has his credentials and his duty weapon in his desk, so we've got time. No need to go off half-cocked."

"Which brings us up to the subject of next moves."

"I'll take the best witness we have in the rape cases and re-interview her. You start looking at the remaining suspects. If Ayers didn't rape the women, and we can prove it, then everyone is going to take our investigation into this shooting with a more open mind."

"Of course we've just added a suspect."

"Nichols."

"Exactly. If he deliberately killed Ayers, then he might have killed Angie Maitland. And one possible motive might be to put the rape cases to bed once and for all."

"Okay." Pete looked at his watch. "I've got to go. I'm supervising a range class this evening, but I'll turn it over to Hernandez. That way I can get started on the rape interviews. You realize that a whole task force was working on this and now it's just going to be the two of us?"

I sighed. "Plus we have to keep open the possibility that the shooting was motivated by something else. In fact, discreetly looking into Nichols's background is a priority too. Good thing we're both super cops."

"Yeah," he said dryly. "Did I mention the tendonitis in my left arm and the pressure of shepherding two teenage girls through their high school years?" Mentioning his girls caused him to look down at his phone again, which started to vibrate as if on cue.

I headed for the door. "I'm going to pull the reports on the other rape suspects. I'll take them home and probably do some interviews this weekend."

"I'll work on the rest of the witness statements this weekend too. The girls are going to be out of town, so I'll have time. Call me tomorrow and we'll decide if we want to team up for anything. It would have been horrible for me to have the house all to myself this weekend with nothing to do," Pete said sarcastically, his fingers tapping away at his phone.

I picked up the bulk of the hardcopy suspect files from the rape cases and asked Dad's assistant to email me the reports from the task force. Then I made a quick call to Cara, who agreed to come over for dinner and insisted that she didn't mind spending the evening watching me read reports.

I had one more unpleasant task before I could call it a day. I sat in my car and dialed the number for Eddie, my cross-dressing snitch. I wanted to catch him before he went on a lost weekend.

"Hey, I've been thinking of you," he greeted me.

"I bet you have. Need money for the weekend?"

"You cut me deeply." Eddie sounded positively buoyant. *He's already started on his weekend,* I thought.

"Yeah, we're such good friends. Look, I'm going to text you a picture. I want to know if you've seen the guy in the foreground next to me."

I selected the picture and sent it to him. Thanks to rural cell service, it took a couple of minutes during which I had to make small talk with Eddie.

"Think it's here," he finally said. "Hey, yeah, I got it. Damn ugly bunch. Especially the guy on the left," he said, trying to make a joke. I was the guy on the left. *Ha, ha.*

"Concentrate, Eddie. The guy next to me. Have you seen

him coming and going from your family's businesses?" It was a picture of a group of us at a department lunch. I'd had to sit next to Matt and Pete had managed to snap a picture and send it to me as a joke.

"Maybe. But I don't think he's a regular. There's something familiar about him, though. Yeah, no." Eddie hemmed and hawed.

"Okay, big help, thanks."

"Did you want to talk in person?" Eddie asked, no doubt hoping that he could pry a twenty out of my wallet.

"Not today. Have a great weekend, Eddie."

"If you're sure."

"I am. Bye, Eddie."

CHAPTER ELEVEN

I slept in late enough the next morning that the sun coming in through my window woke me up. When I opened my eyes I couldn't help but smile. A double window looked out onto my yard where the live oak trees were draped in Spanish moss. I loved that view and hoped to build a house one day that would take full advantage of it. But this morning the view was even better. Cara was standing at the window looking out at the trees. She wore a large T-shirt and nothing else, her red hair glowing in the morning sunlight. Even with the frost on the ground, the image warmed my heart.

"Good morning," I said softly.

She turned toward me with a huge smile on her face. "I didn't think you'd ever wake up."

"I would have woken up sooner if I'd known how beautiful the world was going to be," I said with an idiotic grin on my face.

She came toward the bed and I thought for a moment that the morning was going to be perfect, but then the mood was broken by the sounds of running, hissing and gruff little barks. Alvin, Cara's Pug, jumped up on the bed and turned to face his nemesis, but he was too slow and Ivy was already up and after him. He scrambled, trying to hide behind me.

73

"Ivy, that's not a very nice way to treat a guest."

The nine-pound tabby cat turned and gave me a cold stare, telling me to mind my own business. I put my hand out to her. I thought she was going to reject the offer, but ear scratchies were too good to pass up. Alvin decided that his life had been spared and laid down carefully next to me, keeping a close eye on his feline attacker.

Cara sat next to us on the bed. Ivy allowed her one pet before stalking off.

"I guess she doesn't care much for sleepovers," Cara said, leaning over and giving me a quick kiss before heading to the bathroom.

"Well, she'll just have to get used to it."

We fed Alvin and Ivy before getting ourselves some cereal.

"Guess you have work to do?" Cara said.

"Sorry."

"It's all right. I just hate that I'm going to miss spending one of my free Saturdays with you." The vet's office was open every other Saturday.

"Maybe we can plan something for the weekend after next."

She perked up. "Like what?"

"I don't know. The beach?" I suggested.

"That would be nice. There's something about the beach in winter. It seems more wild and primitive."

"Fewer people too," I said.

"More romantic."

"I like the way you think," I said, getting up from the table. I knew I shouldn't, but I figured Ivy deserved a treat and gave her the rest of the milk in my bowl. My reward was the first purr from her since Cara and Alvin had arrived last night.

Cara followed me into the bedroom as I got ready to go.

"What're you going to be doing?"

"I want to check on the other potential suspects the rape task force was considering. Saturday seems like a good day to catch some of them at home. And the sooner we clear this up, the better for the department and Dad."

"Do you think you'll want to get together for dinner?"

I was filling my pockets with keys, wallet and change. "You bet." I clipped on my phone, badge and gun and came over and kissed her.

"Mind if I just stay here today?" Cara asked. It sounded like she expected me to say no.

"I don't mind at all." It actually made me feel good inside to think that I'd come home to a full house. Not that Ivy wasn't good company. "Of course, you'd better ask the mistress of the Macklin estate." I pointed to Ivy, who was staring at us from the doorway. A soft, submissive bark came from the living room. "Alvin might not be too keen on the idea either."

I left my place feeling wonderful. I had no idea that it would be all downhill from there.

I pulled up in front of a brick home that looked like it had been built in the seventies; a garage had been enclosed more recently. There were two cars and an older, full-size pickup truck parked in the driveway. I pulled up behind the truck. The yard was neat and the house had the look of belonging to an older couple, with miniature white picket fences around the flowerbeds and everything neat and well painted. Smoke was coming from the chimney. This was Ethan Girard's parents' home.

My knock was answered by a middle-aged woman with salt-and-pepper shoulder-length hair and more than her share of what my grandmother used to call worry wrinkles. The wrinkles deepened when she frowned at my badge.

"Mrs. Girard?"

"Yes."

"I'd like to talk to Ethan."

"You all should leave him alone. He hasn't done…"

She was interrupted by her husband coming up behind

her. He was stout with a large pot belly. His eyes went down to my badge. "Just let him in." He turned his head and yelled, "Ethan!"

Mr. and Mrs. Girard made way for me, but neither one of them took their eyes off of me.

"You can talk in there." Mr. Girard pointed toward a dining table that sat off to the side of the kitchen in a small alcove.

A man of about thirty, wearing sweat pants, a T-shirt and socks, came out of the back of the house. His eyes zeroed in on me and he shook his head.

"What the hell?"

"Watch your language," his father said in a tone that suggested correcting his son was routine. He turned and left the two of us alone.

"This is just a follow-up interview," I reassured Ethan.

He dropped down onto a chair and sulked. He looked like a shorter, thinner version of his father.   I took out a pad and a small recorder as I sat down across from him.

"I thought the guy that raped those women was dead," Ethan said, head down and staring at the flowery tablecloth.

"That's a possibility, but we want to make sure that we haven't missed anything."

He looked up sharply. "What, like pinning something on me?"

"Like I said, we just want to make sure that we can close out these cases knowing that we got the right man. Reading over your file, it doesn't look like anyone *pinned* anything on you in the past. Two convictions for sexual assault. You pleaded guilty on both of them." I wanted to make sure he understood who was in charge of this interview.

His eyes went back to the tablecloth. "That's right. And it was six years ago when I was drinking. I haven't taken a drink since I went into prison."

"Being drunk just means that your inhibitions were down, and you did what you wanted to do, drunk or sober."

His eyes flashed back at me. There was a mix of anger

and frustration in them now. "I did five years in prison. I've kept to my twelve-step program. I've done a year of therapy. I don't want to rape women. I never wanted to rape women."

"I'm not here to rake you over the coals, but let's be honest. Honesty, isn't that one of the values that the twelve-step program encourages? You *did* rape those women. I accept that you did your time and the reports from your parole officer indicate that you're staying straight. But with your record, and the fact that you knew two of the women that were attacked in the last month, are you surprised that we're interested in you as a suspect?" I asked reasonably.

"No. But that doesn't make it right. I did know Elaine pretty well. She worked at the restaurant with me." He paused and sighed. "Where I used to work. You know they fired me? Laid me off, what a laugh. It was two days after you all talked to me the first time. Wonder what made Mr. Heron decide to fire me…"

"And the other girl?" I asked, ignoring him.

"I didn't even know her name. She lives a block over. My parents were friends with her parents. Guess what? Not anymore."

"Linda. Her name's Linda Evers." His self pity was wearing thin on me. Yes, it's tough when you are trying to go straight and your past haunts you, but…

"Yeah, Linda. You read my file. When I… assaulted those girls it was… I took them on a date, got drunk and forced myself on them. It was different."

I had to admit I'd thought the same thing when he'd came up as a suspect originally. Rapists often have one MO and they stick to it. The method is part of the thrill. Of course, like serial killers, serial rapists' methods can evolve.

"Tell me where you were on Wednesday night."

"The night the woman got killed and the guy was shot?" He seemed genuinely surprised to be asked about it.

"Yes, this Wednesday from about nine to midnight."

"I went to a meeting and came home. It's not like I got a

job."

"Where and what time was the meeting?"

"Nine o'clock at the First Baptist Church. Not my favorite meeting, but I've had to go back every night since I got fired. I left about eleven and came home."

"You came directly home?"

"No, wait, I stopped for a Red Bull at the Fast Mart. That's it. Came home and played *War Age* online for a couple of hours."

I made notes. It could all be checked. Who was actually playing the online game could be a question, but if he went to the Fast Mart after the meeting that would pretty much eliminate him.

"We'll check out your alibi."

"It is what it is," he said.

I turned off the recorder and got up. "Good luck with staying sober," I said sincerely. The guy was pathetic, but if he could stay sober it would be good for everyone.

CHAPTER TWELVE

Next on the list was my prime suspect for the rapes. David Conway was the youngest suspect we'd interviewed, and I think that's what had persuaded some of the other members of the task force not to take him seriously. But I'd sat in on the formal interview with him. He had a cold, dispassionate attitude that he could change like a chameleon to warm and personable. It was subtle and chilling to watch.

On paper, his history looked less ominous than Ethan's. Conway had been arrested twice for "sexually interfering" with several girls when he was in high school. I had also managed to find two incident reports from his time at the University of Florida, when he was warned about peeping in dorm windows. This suggested that he'd had some maturity issues and gotten over them. But watching and listening to him, all I could think was that he had simply gotten more clever.

After the interview I had searched crime reports from Gainesville, with a little help from a friend with the Alachua County Sheriff's Office, and came up with several rapes that seemed similar to ours. But, sadly, rape is not an unusual crime near a college campus. I had to admit that I could probably search the records of any large college town for the same period and come up with an equal number of cases. The MO wasn't that unusual either. That's where our investigation of Conway had stalled.

Like Ethan Girard, David Conway lived with his parents, but on the other side of the county. It was almost noon, so I decide to stop for a quick lunch at Winston's Grill before making the drive. I called Cara while I waited for Mary to bring my order.

"I'm taking a lunch break."

"Where at?"

"Winston's."

"Let me guess... The barbecue wrap?" Cara asked, referring to a recent addition to the menu that I'd become instantly addicted to.

"That isn't even worth five points," I kidded her and was rewarded with the sound of laughter. "Sure is a beautiful day," I said, looking out the window at the bright blue winter sky.

"I wish I was with you."

"Me too. I'm going to talk with Conway, then I'll do one more and be done. Maybe we'll get lucky and they won't be home."

"I'll keep my fingers crossed."

"How are Alvin and Ivy getting along?"

"They're both crashed in separate sunbeams, so I'm sharing the peace and quiet with a good book."

"I'll let you know when I'm headed your direction."

David Conway's father, Mel, owned a small production company in Tallahassee that made most of its money off of commercials. The Conways were some of the many people that had chosen to live in Adams County to take advantage of the cheaper taxes, rural setting and half hour commute to Tallahassee. The road they lived on had twenty or thirty newly built, upper-middle class homes sitting on at least five acres each.

The Conways' Federal style two-story house was set back from the road, but close enough that it could be seen and admired by anyone driving by. I parked in the circular driveway. A red pickup truck with a topper was parked in front of the garage.

Knocking on the door and ringing the bell didn't bring any response. I went back to my car and checked David Conway's file. The pickup belonged to him. I knocked on the door again without any luck. On a whim, I tried turning the knob and the door opened. *Odd. Is he hiding?* I wondered. Even out here no one leaves their door unlocked when they're not at home.

I stood back and looked at the house. Turning around, I noticed a couple uncollected newspapers by the front gate.

Should I go in? The law was a little fuzzy here. *Could I claim that I had a compelling reason? Was concerned for the occupant's safety?* Maybe, but the best course would be to walk around the house and look for further evidence that would make any reasonable person concerned enough to enter the house.

I started around the side of the house. The lawn was neat and tidy. Hedges made it a chore to get in close enough to peek through the windows, but I managed to do it while getting snagged and poked by the holly bushes. The windows were shut tight. I could see a few lights on, but nothing looked out of place. Then halfway around the side of the house I caught the first whiff.

I gave up on the windows and started following the smell. It seemed to be coming from the back of the house where I could see a screened-in pool. The odor was much stronger now. *Is it time for the radio or the gun?* the cop part of my brain asked. Whatever it was had been dead a while. The smell was worse than any dead body I'd ever encountered and that was saying a lot.

When I could see the entire pool area I noticed a glass on the side of the hot tub. Reluctantly, I made my way to the screen door. The odor was almost a physical barrier now. I had to force myself to open the door and go near the hot tub.

What I saw made my whole body convulse. I ran outside

to a nearby flowerbed, falling down in the plants as I vomited until my stomach was empty. Finally, I was able to call in the dead body that was boiling in a stew of its own flesh.

Cops, firefighters, EMTs and morticians all deal with death through the liberal use of black humor and Vick's Vapor Rub. But today no one made snide remarks or crude jokes. I wouldn't have thought it was possible, but this scene was too gruesome. No amount of vapor rub under the nose could quite wipe out the stench of boiled flesh. Everyone just wanted to get their jobs done, go home and get under a hot shower.

"Dr. Darzi's here," Pete told me. I was leaning against a pine tree, well upwind of the hot tub.

"Bet he loved getting called out on a Saturday."

"Actually, he looked pretty excited," Pete said. I gave him a hard look. "I'm serious. Guess he gets tired of the same old car accidents, stabbings and shootings. Me, on the other hand, you could have left off your call list. Not that I wasn't working anyway."

"How were the interviews going?"

"I talked with two of the women. Neither of them had anything new to add, and I felt like shit for asking them to think about it again. But they both said they'd call me if they thought of anything else."

He nodded toward the pool. "You think this was our suspect?"

"How the hell do I know?" I grumbled, irrationally irritated by the question.

"Yeah, what a mess."

"Sorry. I went through the house while I was waiting on everyone. No one else is here. I didn't find a cell phone or any indication of where the other occupants are."

"The only thing for sure is that it was only one body in the tub. And the hair was short."

"Yeah. I'm figuring it was male, but…" I shrugged. "Guess we ought to go back over there," I said reluctantly and started back.

Within a hundred feet of the enclosure there was no safety in being upwind. *Will the smell ever come out of this place?* I wondered. I could see Dr. Darzi, wearing a hazmat suit, carefully fishing around in the tub. They had raised the body, or at least what was left of it, out of the water and laid it on a huge plastic sheet that was draped over a stretcher. A camera on a tripod was focused on the hot tub, making a gruesome record of the recovery of the body and its parts. I could see Shantel and Marcus bagging and tagging items around the pool deck.

Darzi finally lifted something small and square out of the water. A cell phone. One of his assistants came forward with a plastic evidence bag and Darzi dropped the phone into it. He noticed me and stood up, waving.

When he was standing next to Pete and me, he took off his helmet and mask. "What a gruesome discovery you made."

"Can you tell us anything?" I asked.

"It's a male. Between the ages of seventeen and thirty-five would be my guess. Most of the skin has sloughed off, which makes it hard to tell if he has any bruising, cuts or ligature marks. His hair is brown and he's five-foot ten, roughly. Normal weight. Be very glad he wasn't overweight or this would have been much worse."

"That's hard to imagine," Pete said.

"Believe me, if the tub had been filled with fat… far worse. As it is, one of my interns threw up." He pointed to the area in the flowerbed where I'd lost my lunch. "He got to the same place you did. Trying to keep it all together. And you all weren't the only ones."

"Anything else?" I asked, trying to move the subject away from retching lest I start dry-heaving again. As it was, I was never going to be able to eat one of Winston's barbecue wraps again.

"When we get the parts back to the morgue, I'll be able to tell you a bit more. A toxin screen will give us blood alcohol and drug levels. We'll be able to determine if he was stabbed or shot." He shrugged.

"I'd appreciate…" I started.

He held up his hand. "You don't need to tell me to put a rush on it. We have to autopsy a body in this condition as quickly as possible."

"Can you give us an approximate time of death?"

"A couple of days? The temperature of the water was one hundred and eighteen degrees. I know a researcher at the body farm in Tennessee. I'll give him a call and see if they have any data that can help me narrow it down. But I think we'll be lucky to put it in a twenty-four-hour window. Unlike a body out in the open, insects couldn't get to our victim. And insects are one of our best clues once we're beyond what the body's temperature can tell us." He was sounding a bit like the college lecturer he was on some days.

"I know you'll do your best."

"We did recover a phone."

"So we might get an earliest possible time of death from it."

"Ha, can't wait to see the IT folks when they unbag that little stink bomb," Pete said.

"Yeah, I might warn them," I offered. "We really need the numbers off of it."

"Tallahassee police are helping us track down someone from," Pete looked down at his phone, "Rambling Oaks Productions, the Conways' company, to get a contact number for the parents."

"If his parents can provide dental records, it will be faster than DNA. If it's their son, that is," Darzi said.

"We'll follow up on that as soon as we find the parents."

CHAPTER THIRTEEN

An hour later we had a number for Mel Conway. I dialed, got voicemail and left a message for a call back as soon as possible. Five minutes after I hung up, my phone rang.

"Conway here, what's up?" He sounded suspicious.

"I'm Deputy Macklin, an investigator with the Adams County Sheriff's Office." I'd tried to think of the best way to put the rest of what I had to tell him. Not knowing if it was his son, I decided to proceed with caution. "I'm checking on the welfare of your family, Mr. Conway. Could you tell me where your wife and son are?"

"What do you mean you're checking on their welfare? My wife is right here with me."

"And where are you?"

"What the hell is this all about?"

"Please bear with me. We're trying to figure this out too."

"We're in Panama City. We just finished filming a commercial. Figure out what?"

"And your son?"

"Hard to say with him. He's supposed to be at home watching the place. What's happened? Has our house burned down or something? That would be just like him."

"Mr. Conway, you need to come home. We found a body

at your house. We haven't identified it yet. It might not be your son," I told him, but the odds seemed to be going up that it was.

"You don't know?" Conway's voice was shaky. "There are pictures of him in the house."

"I'm afraid the body isn't recognizable." I didn't want to go into the horrid details on the phone.

"I see."

"If you could come home immediately, that would be a great help. However, you'll want to arrange to stay with friends or at a hotel. I'm afraid your house is currently designated as a crime scene." Gee, was there any other bad news I could give him?

"I see," he repeated, then went quiet for a moment or two. "Okay, I can leave all of this to be packed up by Edgar. Maya and I can be there in a couple hours." I looked at my watch. Two hours would put them back at eight o'clock.

"I'll meet you at your house," I told him, hanging up.

I'd texted Cara earlier and told her I'd be running late. Now I figured I didn't have any choice but to call her. I didn't want to call her, because I knew that the best thing would be for her to go home. I wouldn't be in any mood to be sociable when I got home, which probably wouldn't be until ten at least. I sighed and called.

"Hey! Where are you?" she asked cheerily.

"I found a body. And now I'm waiting for the parents, who are down in Panama City and won't be here for another couple of hours."

"That sucks. Is there anything I can do?"

"Honestly, you might as well go home."

"Why?" She sounded hurt, which seemed unfair. I just wanted to spare her from my foul mood.

"Because I'm not going to be much fun when I do get home."

"I don't care about that."

"Well, I do."

"I don't mind…"

"Cara, I've had a shitty day. I just want to go to bed when I get home," I said more harshly than I meant to.

My mind was going over all of the plates I was juggling: whatever the hell was going on with Matt; the rapist that might or might not still be on the loose; Deputy Nichols, who was lying to us about shooting Ayers; all the political fallout that was going to come down on Dad; and now this horrific death. I just wanted to have some time where I didn't have to think... about anything.

"We don't have to talk. I'm happy to just be with—"

I couldn't argue with her about this anymore. I couldn't think of a way to explain it to her without hurting her feelings, so I did the obvious thing and hurt her feelings.

"Just go home," I said, and instantly felt the cold chill come through the cell phone. "I'll talk to you tomorrow," I added hastily, already feeling like crap.

"Okay then. Bye." She hung up before I could say anything more.

I stared at my phone, wondering what I should do. I was too frustrated and tired to call her back, even though not calling was going to eat at me.

I looked up to see Pete walking toward me, texting at the same time.

"What's wrong? Besides all the obvious," he asked. Then he saw the dejected look on my face as I put away my phone. "Oh, new relationship angst."

"Not in the mood," I growled.

He held up his hands in surrender. "We've got time to catch some dinner before the parents get here."

"You've got to be kidding me." My stomach wasn't even close to ready for food. But Pete had almost three hundred pounds to nourish and one sautéed dead body wasn't going to put him off.

"I hear you. Look, I'll go and bring you something back... Maybe some crackers? A PowerBar? You got to eat something or you're going to collapse. And you better put on a heavier coat too."

I realized that I could see his breath. "Okay, just bring me back a Coke and a couple PowerBars."

After he left I went back and stood outside the pool enclosure where Shantel and Marcus were almost finished collecting evidence. The sun had fallen below the horizon and the area was lit by the house's exterior spotlights and the crime scene work lights. I watched as Marcus made a final sweep of the pool deck and Shantel continued to fish in the murky soup at the bottom of the hot tub. They had managed to find the drain on the pump, but the last four or five inches of disgusting muck refused to drain out.

Shantel stood up suddenly, something small gripped in her glove, then washed the item off in the bucket of fresh water they had for that purpose. She held the item up to the camera before she put it in an evidence bag. Spotting me, she came through the screen door and headed my direction.

The smell reached me when she was still twenty feet away. I held up my hand.

"I'm sorry, but that's close enough," I told her.

Shantel took off her helmet and almost retched when the full force of the odor hit her. "Oh, Jesus, save me," she said. She held out the bag in her hand. Then, realizing I was serious about not letting her get any closer, she set it on the ground. I took out my flashlight and approached the bag, waving her back.

"The odor's not that bad," Shantel said. I gave her the eye. "Okay, it's pretty horrible. Guess I've got to go back to the office and get a shower before I go home," she said, shaking her head. "Oh, that's a ring. I found it at the bottom of the hot tub. Leon High School class ring. His name is on the inside."

I stopped looking at the ring. "Why show it to me if you're just going to tell me everything about it?"

"Well, ain't you in the mood tonight? Hey, I'm out here too. I'm not exactly enjoying spending a Saturday night fishing around in human muck for the department." Shantel never let anyone give her lip.

"Sorry. This hasn't been a good week and this is pretty much the icing on the cake. Not the ring. The body."

"Tell me about it." Shantel kept her ear close to the tracks and always knew what was going on in the department. "I know the sheriff's in for a hard ride. But he'll get through it."

She had a fondness for Dad, who had recognized her and Marcus as the unsung heroes of our crime scene unit. He never hesitated to give them the credit they deserved and, more to the point, he made sure they got a salary that would keep them happy and on the job.

"Rumor has it that you've found a girl who'll go out with you," Shantel kidded me. The look on my face must have told her all she needed to know. "Oh, so it's like that."

"It's like nothin'," I told her.

"She does what? Works for Dr. Barnhill? It's hard to be the SO of a cop or a fireman. Takes a lot of patience. Not many women are happy to learn that a job comes before them."

"I told you, it's not... Well, maybe it *is* like that, but it's complicated," I said, trying not to be too prickly with Shantel. Something I should have worked harder on when I was talking to Cara.

"No, honey, it's not complicated. You're a deputy and you want to be with a woman, so you got to work twice as hard as a man with a normal job." She stuck her hand up to stop me replying. "That's all I'm going to say."

I thanked her for the ring. She helped Marcus pack up and they left before Pete got back, leaving me sitting all alone in the cold, hungry and covered in the stench of death. Oh, yeah, I had myself a little pity party. Even when you know it's stupid, counterproductive and selfish, sometimes it's hard not to feel sorry for yourself. Tonight, on top of everything else, I was feeling bad for being a jerk. But deep down there was a dumbass telling me that I had a right to be a jerk. I was glad to see Pete drive up so I could quit talking to myself.

CHAPTER FOURTEEN

We were sitting in my car with the heat running when the Conways' SUV came up the drive. I took a last swallow of Coke and we got out to meet them

"Can we go inside?" Mel Conway asked.

"Of course. But we can't let you move about in the house by yourselves. We'll be done with the house and grounds by Monday afternoon or Tuesday. But if you want to get anything this evening, we'll be glad to help you."

"I just want to use the restroom and have something to drink," Conway said, looking at his wife, who just nodded.

Pete and I followed them into the house. It was a half hour before we were all seated around the kitchen table.

"I don't understand," Maya Conway said, sounding confused and frightened. She was petite with an olive complexion and straight black hair. I'd learned from the DMV information I'd pulled up on them that she was over fifty, but looking at her I would have guessed much younger.

"We can't be positive that the body we found is your son's until we've had a chance to compare his dental records or, barring that, compared his DNA."

"Couldn't we see him? Surely we can tell you if it's our son," Mel offered. We had tried to avoid going into details about the condition of the body.

"You don't want to see the body," I said firmly, looking squarely into Mr. Conway's eyes. He flinched, but took my meaning.

"We did find a ring with the body."

Both of the Conways looked at me as though I was going to throw them a life preserver. Evidence that this was someone else's nightmare. I pulled out the bag and set it on the table. Both of them reached for it at the same time.

"Don't open the bag," I said. I didn't really think the ring had an ounce of trace evidence on it, after what it had been through, but I didn't want them opening the bag and letting the smell of death into the room.

When they looked at the ring their faces told me everything I needed to know.

"The ring wasn't found on the body." I hated myself for giving them hope that was almost surely false.

"He always wore that ring," his father said in a tone flat with shock.

"How could this have happened?" Maya Conway asked everyone and no one at the same time.

"Right now we don't know much."

"He took drugs sometimes. Bought drugs," Mel said.

"What type of drugs was he taking?" Pete asked, his voice calm and sympathetic.

"Nothing really. Pot, a little pot, and I think cocaine." His mother was used to defending him.

"Amphetamines sometimes too. We got him into rehab once."

"It was recreational. He could hold down a job."

"Could. He just wouldn't. So this was probably an accident?" Mel Conway asked us.

"Really, we don't know yet. Was anyone else supposed to be here at the house while you were gone?" I asked.

"No. Shouldn't have been. I told him I didn't want any of his friends, and I use that term loosely, staying here. Actually, that was one thing he was pretty good about. He didn't like

91

people messing with his stuff, so he tended to keep people at a distance."

"David doesn't party much." His mother took every opportunity to mention the good things about him.

"Always been a loner, really." His father, on the other hand, seemed to paint every trait in the darkest colors.

"Do you know of anyone that might have wanted to hurt your son?" When I said it, I expected the usual denials that you get from parents. I wasn't prepared for the angry look I got from Mrs. Conway.

"David didn't have any enemies until you all started accusing him of those rapes!" she said venomously.

"We never charged him with anything." I felt myself go on the defensive.

"Your lot were asking questions everywhere. People knew what you thought. We moved here to get away from all those nasty things people said about him, but you couldn't let him be."

"In fairness, your son *was* a registered sex offender," Pete told her. "That information is public."

"There, that's what I mean." Her eyes were hot coals now, her voice rising.

"They're right." Mel Conway put his hand on his wife's arm. "He did some awful things when he was a teenager." Conway looked me in the eyes. "But you all did stir things up. He hadn't been in that kind of trouble for over six years. And Maya's right. There were people who said things. I was in the Supersave and heard the manager say that sex offenders should be neutered. He said it on purpose. He knew I was there."

"My son didn't do those rapes. And you found that out." Maya hadn't cooled down much. "You all killed the man who did it."

"Can you think of any other reason that someone might have wanted to hurt your son?" Pete asked, trying to steer the conversation in a more productive direction.

"No. Like I said, most of the time he just hung around

here since he hasn't been able to get a job. Not that he was trying too hard to find one."

"When was the last time you talked to your son?"

"I talked to him Wednesday when we were having lunch," Maya said, her anger turning back to grief.

"We went down to Panama City on Sunday," Mel Conway added.

"Was there anything unusual about the call?" I asked.

"No. David had just gotten up. He wasn't really in a mood to talk."

"Everything sounded okay?"

She glanced at her husband and said, "He asked for money. And I told him that I had some in my bedside table. Nothing more."

"Do you mind if we look around David's room?" I asked. I'd walked through the house after I discovered the body, but since we didn't yet know how he died, we'd have been on very shaky ground if we had conducted a more thorough search. Until Dr. Darzi was able to decide the cause of death, it was reasonable for us to keep the house closed as a crime scene, but to do more without the Conways' permission would give a lawyer a wide open door for getting evidence excluded.

"It was probably an accident. We've told you he used drugs. Couldn't he have fallen asleep and drowned?"

"Of course," I had to admit.

"Then I don't think you need to search his room." Mel Conway didn't sound like he could be persuaded.

"It is also possible that someone killed your son. And until the autopsy, we are going to keep the house preserved as a crime scene." I tried to sound equally determined.

"Fair enough."

"When can we have him back?" his mother pleaded. I realized that all of us were assuming that the body was David.

"After the autopsy. The coroner will perform the autopsy tomorrow. If it is your son, the body could be released to you as early as Monday. If you can give us the name of your son's dentist, we'll contact him and get the dental records. If we have to wait for the DNA tests, it could be a week or more."

"Dr. Wilde in Tallahassee. We've used him since David was in middle school."

Pete and I watched them while they gathered up fresh clothes, then we escorted them out to their SUV. Mr. Conway told us they were staying at a hotel in Tallahassee and to call them if we needed more information or had any news. He had an eerie way of switching from grieving father to professional businessman in the span of a sentence.

Pete and I followed them out of the driveway and I stopped to put a departmental chain and padlock on the gate, along with a sign declaring it a crime scene.

Ivy was waiting for me when I got home, indignantly demanding her dinner. I was too drained to wallow in the silence of my trailer, and crawled into bed with my nightmares until the sun came up.

CHAPTER FIFTEEN

I awoke to Ivy kneading my chest. It was almost nine o'clock. There were two messages on my phone, one from Dad and the other from Dr. Darzi. Dad's simply said: *Call me.* I knew that he would want a full report on what had gone on at Conway's. Darzi's message was equally brief: *Autopsy at noon.* The message had been sent to Pete too. I was trying to decide if I could talk him into going without me when the phone rang: Dad's gunshot ring tone.

"I was going to call you."

"It's almost nine-thirty."

"Yep, that's what my phone says. Is that all you wanted to tell me?" I tried to sound lighthearted, but I wasn't in the mood.

"I want to know what went on at Conway's house." Clearly he wasn't in a joking mood either.

"I've got to go to the autopsy at noon. I want to grab some breakfast, then I'll stop by your house on the way to the hospital."

"Fine." Then as an afterthought he added, "How are you doing?"

"I'll survive."

"I talked to Shantel. She said it was the worst body she'd

ever seen."

"It was bad." He'd inadvertently managed to destroy my appetite.

"See you when you get here," he said and hung up.

I called Pete and arranged to meet him at the office so we could ride over to the autopsy together. Pete had already gotten in touch with Dr. Wilde, who'd agreed to drop off David Conway's dental records with Dr. Darzi.

Now I was left staring at my phone, knowing I needed to send a text to Cara, but not sure what to say. It was cowardly to not even consider calling. I justified it by telling myself that if I texted her, I was giving her a chance to respond when she was ready instead of ambushing her with a phone call.

I decided on the classic: *I'm sorry about last night. It was a very bad day. Hope you'll forgive me.* I figured that was groveling enough.

Her response was immediate. A good sign? *Not mad. Let's talk when you have the time.*

I couldn't decide if the message absolved me or if I should have been worried about the upcoming "talk." One of the things I liked most about Cara was that she was straightforward and honest, so I decided to take the message at face value and try to feel better about things.

At Dad's house, Mauser came bounding out to meet me and led me to the back of the house where Dad was working on his patio. He'd started it shortly before Mom died and since then it had become a gauge of his stress level. It was already large; now it looked like it would soon need its own zip code.

"I'm putting in a brick grill," he said as I stared at the mess he'd created. "Let's go inside."

Mauser seemed reluctant to trade the cold winter air for the warmth of the house, but he didn't want to be left outside alone so he pushed past me and into the house. I was forced to battle him for a small section of the couch.

I brought Dad up to speed on where we were with

Nichols, then recounted the events of yesterday. Dad knew most of the story from monitoring the radio, and he'd talked to Pete at one point early on.

"Hopefully Dr. Darzi will be able to give us a cause of death and the approximate time, or at least day, of death," I said, shoving Mauser's big butt off my lap.

Dad got up and waved his hand for me to follow. I was more than glad to abandon the battlefield of the couch to Mauser. Dad led me to the spare bedroom, which had been Mom's hobby room. Inside he'd laid out several boxes' worth of files in neat piles. He'd labeled them with either the names of suspects or victims.

"I've cross-referenced them," he said, pointing to a whiteboard where he'd made connections between the suspects and the crimes. "With these cases, it's hard to tell the good guys from the bad guys. We have the murder of Angie Maitland and the shooting of Jeffrey Ayers. Now I've added the death of David Conway."

"Might be too early to put Conway's death up with the rest."

"You mean it's too soon to assume that the body is Conway's?" Dad asked.

"No. I'm pretty sure that it's Conway's body. But don't you think it might be too soon to put it in the middle of a grand conspiracy?"

"I don't. I know that coincidences do happen. And if he'd died two weeks after the shooting incident, or even a week, I might be able to see them as separate events. But to happen within a day? Whether before or after. Like you said, hopefully the autopsy will tell us. But that close together, I think it's safe to say that they're linked."

"We believe that Matt is involved with the Thompsons, but we don't know of any connections between him and these crimes." I waved my hand at the piles.

"True. I'm not as sure about him being tied into this as I am that the death of Conway is linked. And where the hell does Nichols fit into all this?"

"You know that you can trust Pete, and there are others in the department too," I argued.

"But if I tell them… If I tell them our assumptions and show them the facts we have, it would put them in an awkward position."

"Pete already thinks that there is something hinky about the Ayers shooting," I pushed.

"Which is good, and that's another reason to keep him in the dark. If he makes the links independently, then we know we're on the right track. I want him to remain unbiased."

That actually made sense. Dad could be very persuasive. If he started preaching his theories to Pete or anyone else, he might just sway them based on his powers of argument rather than the evidence.

The sound of whining came from the hallway. Dad had shut the door and now Mauser was feeling left out.

"We're coming out!" Dad shouted to him, then turned back to me. "I wanted to show this to you so you can think about it while you're out in the field. I'm going to rely on your instincts."

I realized again how he'd talked me into becoming a deputy against my better judgment. Dad's faith in me was a strong motivating force in my life, but I just wasn't sure if it was a good thing or a bad thing.

"I've got to go meet Pete for the autopsy," I said, and opened the door to an aggrieved Mauser, now sulking on the floor.

"I know you'll be broken-hearted about this, but I started without you," Dr. Darzi said, not looking up from the ugliest corpse I'd ever seen. The hours in the hot tub had left the body looking like one of those white, swollen grub worms. The odor was still bad, but not as overwhelming as when the body had been swimming in its own heated juices.

I glanced at Pete, who looked as pale and queasy as I felt. "Did you get the dental records?" he asked.

"Yes, and I already X-rayed his teeth," Darzi said. As if on cue, an assistant came in and began pulling up, clicking and moving things on a computer. A series of images appeared side by side on a set of monitors on one wall.

"They appear to match, Doctor," the young man said as he moved one digital X-ray over another. Darzi stopped working over the body and went over for a closer look at the dental images.

"Yes, I can say with no doubt that this is David Conway." *One question answered*, I thought.

"Time of death?"

Darzi gave me a frown. "Don't rush me. Actually, that is easier than cause of death. From the condition of the musculature and the skin, or the lack of skin, the data from the body farm suggests that he was submerged in the tub for at least forty-eight hours, and no more than seventy-two. So sometime between Wednesday afternoon and Thursday afternoon." He held up his hand to stop me. "Cause of death. Much harder." He went back to the body.

"Can you rule anything out?" Pete asked.

"One, he doesn't have any broken bones. Two, there is very little liquid in his lungs, so I don't think he drowned. Three, his windpipe is intact, so he probably wasn't strangled. Four, the X-ray didn't show any foreign objects in his body. So no bullets or anything stuffed down or up an orifice.

"What I can't tell you is if he was beaten without breaking any bones, and I'm still checking for stab wounds or punctures. Remember that something with the diameter of an ice pick could be used to kill someone. With the body swollen like it is, it's going to be almost impossible to find a small incision or puncture. I'm going to dry the body out and see if that helps us find something, but I can't guarantee anything."

"What are your 'we-won't-hold-you-to-them' thoughts?" I pressed.

Darzi shrugged. "If it was an accident, then it was

probably caused by heat stress or drug overdose. The two could even have augmented each other. Natural causes could be heart failure or aneurysm, rare in young men, but possible."

He stopped and looked at Pete and me. "Of course, what you are most interested in is murder. If he was murdered, I would suspect suffocation, drug overdose or poisoning. The condition of the lungs might tell me if he was suffocated, but unfortunately the hot water destroyed his eyes and other possible markers. Toxicology will tell us if drugs were involved, but not whether they were self-administered. If it was poison, the toxicology report will also give us that information."

"What do you think you can learn from him now?" Pete asked.

"As soon as I open his stomach, we will get some answers." Darzi turned back to the body and began making the "Y" incision in Conway's chest. An hour later he was able to tell us that Conway had undigested pizza in his stomach and nothing else.

"No undigested pills. That's something. And nothing in his lungs or airways to suggest that he was suffocated. I think you're stuck until we get the lab reports. Maybe by Friday," Darzi said.

"From what we know or don't know now, wouldn't it be logical to look for evidence of drug use or suicide at the victim's home?" I asked after the proverbial lightbulb came on over my head.

"You always talk about how the evidence beyond the body can be very important when determining a cause of death, if there isn't a clear-cut answer from the autopsy," Pete added, seeing where I was going with this.

Dr. Darzi stared at Pete as though he was seeing him for the first time. "You sound like you read my article in the *University Medical Review.*"

Pete almost blushed. "I did."

"I'm flattered."

"My point being, we would like to acquire a somewhat extensive search warrant for the victim's house, and if you could reinforce our probable cause, that would be very helpful."

"Of course, if it pertains to a possible cause of death."

"Suicide, drug use and murder I think would cover it. We can even include suspicion of involvement in the rapes."

"Exactly, because that could be a motive for suicide or murder," I said.

"Brilliant," Pete said admiringly.

Leaving the morgue with a new sense of purpose, we called the State Attorney and put the request for a warrant in motion. He was a little dubious of the rape link, but was willing to roll with it. He also baulked at the rush aspect, but since we could tell him that people currently resided at the residence and had an expectation that we would clear the matter up as quickly as possible, he agreed to push it through.

We had the warrant by the time we were back in Adams County. I called Mr. Conway.

"I'm sorry to have to tell you, but the coroner confirmed that the body is that of your son." There was never a good way to tell someone that they'd lost a person they loved and cherished. I'd decided that the best course was to simply deliver the news. They didn't want my sympathy and there was never anything I could say to diminish their grief.

"I knew it was him." Conway's tone was flat and emotionless.

"We have a warrant to search your house for evidence that might help to establish the cause of death. You can be present if you'd like."

"I can meet you there in an hour," he said.

CHAPTER SIXTEEN

As Pete drove us back through Calhoun on the way out to the Conways' house, I saw something that made my breath catch in my throat. "Go back around the block!" I shouted at Pete. "Right, here, take a right."

"What, what?" he yelled, skidding a bit into the turn.

"Turn right again. Now go up two blocks. Your reaction time really wasn't great," I kidded him.

"Let's go to the range and we can compare reaction times," Pete shot back.

"I saw Nichols. I want to know what he's up to." I didn't tell him that what had really interested me was the fact that Nichols had been talking with Matt.

Pete turned back onto Jefferson Street. Nichols was standing next to Matt in front of the Deep Pit Bar-B-Que stand.

"What's up?" Pete asked.

"It's okay. I was just wondering who he was talking to."

"Yeah, might be interesting to find out from Matt if Nichols was asking about the investigation."

If he'd tell us, I thought. "It would."

"You should ask him. God knows that jerk won't talk to me," Pete said bitterly. That was another reason I couldn't share our suspicions about Matt with Pete. He wouldn't be able to look at it objectively.

Why was Nichols meeting with Matt? Who had contacted who? Were they both moles within the department? Eddie had said that there was more than one. Of course, they might have just run into each other. My mind spun with all the possibilities, few of them good.

Mel Conway was standing in his driveway, staring at the ground, when we drove up. He didn't say a word as I unlocked the gate and we all walked up to the house.

"If you can keep from making too big of a mess, I'd appreciate it," he said without rancor, once we were inside.

"We aren't going to tear your house apart. We're mostly interested in David's room." I didn't tell him that if we had wanted to do a full search and leave the place a shambles, we'd have brought in more people.

Pete and I went our separate ways, searching the downstairs fairly quickly. We found several beer bottles and glasses that we thought might contain DNA from other people who had visited the house before David died, or who might be involved in his death. Finding nothing else obviously relevant, we headed upstairs.

We'd agreed to search David's room together. Conway led the way. David's room was large, bright and surprisingly neat, though I'd learned over the years that a person's occupation or lifestyle was not necessarily an indicator of their housekeeping skills. I'd been in homes of well-dressed professionals that were absolutely filthy.

"He was always neat," Conway said, echoing my thoughts.

Pete and I searched the room methodically. He went clockwise from the door while I went counterclockwise. Most of the items in the room were things from David's childhood. Even though I knew the sort of person he had grown up to be, it was poignant seeing toys, pictures and trophies from an apparently happy childhood.

Conway sat on the bed and put his head in his hands.

I reached the closet and started pulling things out and searching through them. Finally all that was left was a high shelf above the clothes hangers. I tried to get a look, but I wasn't quite tall enough.

"Mind if I stand on this chair?" I asked Mel Conway. He looked up. I was holding a wooden desk chair. I didn't want to be solely to blame if it broke.

"No, that's fine."

Pete had finished with the rest of the room, so I handed him boxes, games and a suitcase as I took them off the shelf. The suitcase wasn't empty.

Pete went through the boxes and I opened the suitcase. Inside was an odd collection of items: a Coke bottle, a small blue-and-white metal sign that said "$500 Fine," a pen, a newspaper from 2010, a rock and a dozen other equally odd bits and pieces.

"Does any of this mean anything to you?" I asked Conway, who seemed as puzzled as I was.

"No. I don't think I've seen any of it before."

"Is this David's suitcase?"

"One of his. We keep most of our suitcases in the loft above the laundry room."

I glanced at Pete, who gave me a knowing look. Neither of us wanted to say what we were thinking in front of Mel Conway.

"You think they were trophies?" I asked Pete, once we were back in the car. The suitcase was wrapped in plastic, covered in evidence tags and stored in the trunk.

"Oh, yeah. Trick's going to be proving it."

We drove the suitcase to the station. Matt was coming out as we were walking in. What do you say to someone you suspect of treachery?

"Working on a Sunday?" was the only thing I could think of. Pete was lucky since the two of them never exchanged pleasantries anyway.

"Larry," Matt said noncommittally. *Good, no small talk,* I thought. Then he seemed to notice the bagged suitcase for the first time. "Evidence?"

"Yep," I said, copying his laconic style. He didn't press it, but I thought I could feel him staring at our backs as we went into the office.

"You didn't ask him about his meeting with Nichols," Pete said.

"That day's coming."

Pete gave me a strange look. I'd said it a bit more ominously than I should have.

CHAPTER SEVENTEEN

I stopped by Cara's place a couple hours later. Alvin greeted me with a happy, panting face. Cara didn't seem quite so overjoyed.

"Hey," I said, giving her a light kiss which she accepted. "I'm sorry about last night."

"I know. It's not about being sorry. Can we sit down?" She took my hand and guided me to the couch.

"I know that my job is an issue, but—" I started to say, but she stopped me, shaking her head.

"I came to terms with your job. I wouldn't have said I had if I hadn't. What I can't take is being cut off. Everyone has a hard day. I just want you to give me the opportunity to understand what's going on with you."

"I know and I'm sorry. But sometimes when I've had a bad day, I'm going to need to decompress. You've got to remember that my bad day can mean decomposing bodies or someone trying to kill me."

I was feeling pretty confused at this point. On one hand, what she said made sense. Nothing is more irritating than a person who won't tell you what they're upset about. But on the other hand, sometimes not talking about it was a way for me to handle a particularly traumatizing experience.

"I want to be a part of your life. I'm willing to be a part of those experiences."

"But I want you to be spared that. I don't want to associate my life with you with the crap I have to deal with on the job in the real world." I was trying to understand her point of view, but I felt like she wasn't grasping my side of the argument.

"We can't separate it into our world and the real world. I'm out there too. Bad things happen at my job," she argued.

"Not the same level of bad."

"That's not fair," she said, frowning slightly.

"I don't know how to explain it. I want to look at you and not think about what happens on the job," I argued, frustrated.

"But if you keep me out, how can we really be together?" I heard the frustration in her voice too and instead of making me sympathetic, it just irritated me.

"You can't ask me to justify how I feel. I don't want my whole life colored by the stuff I have to deal with at work."

"If you can't integrate your job into your life, then maybe you do have the wrong job," she said with finality in her tone.

I stood up. "We've been over that already. You know why I do what I do, and why I'm not going to give it up right now."

Anger had boiled to the surface. I could see it in her reaction as much as I felt it in mine. "Look, I think I should go. We both need to think this out."

"Okay," she said, staring down at the carpet as I walked over to the door with Alvin at my heels. The little guy seemed to wonder how the evening had gone so wrong. I reached down and gave him a pet before opening the door.

"Call me," I said, but didn't receive an answer.

The next morning the rain was coming down in waves, perfect weather for my mood. I shook off the rain and waved to the deputy sitting at the front desk. *What was his name?* He'd only been with us for a couple of months and had gotten sucker-punched by a drunk the week before, receiving a few broken ribs. The front desk was a pretty common assignment for light-duty work. *Bruce? Ricky?* I had no idea.

I went straight back to the evidence room. Shantel and Marcus were eating pastries and drinking coffee.

"If it ain't Mr. Brighteyes," Shantel said when she saw me. "You look baaaad. Guess I don't have to ask what you did Sunday. Your partner's been burning up our phones telling us how you all spent your time finding work for us. And him with a wife and children and you with a girlfriend. You can't come up with something better to do?" She shook her head sadly.

"Hey, at least we didn't find another body and ruin Sunday too," I said, trying to get in the spirit of the banter.

"Ugggh, you had to remind me of that body. That was worse than anything I've ever seen," Marcus said, looking at his half-eaten pastry and frowning at it before dropping it in the trashcan. That was saying something, since Marcus had spent several years with NYPD before taking early retirement and moving south.

Pete joined us later as I was helping Marcus and Shantel take pictures and samples from all the items in the suitcase, as well as the case itself.

"I'd like you all to keep this quiet," I told them.

"Quiet from who?" Shantel asked.

"From anyone except me, Pete or the sheriff."

"If this *is* Conway's suitcase and these are souvenirs of his assaults then—" Marcus began.

"Then why the hell would Ayers be hanging over a body behind the store and get shot by Nichols?" Shantel asked.

"We just don't want any rumors going around right now." Pete looked at Marcus and Shantel, who both understood all the implications of the suitcase.

"In fact, if you all could run the samples over to the

FDLE lab yourselves, that would probably be best."

"Road trip! No problem," Shantel said, though FDLE was only thirty miles away in Tallahassee.

"Yeah, it'd be awful if you all had to eat lunch over there."

"Strong possibility of that," Marcus said, "since you ruined my breakfast."

Back at our desks, Pete and I printed out pictures of all the objects. We took them to the conference room where we would have some privacy, and divided them up between us. We wanted to try to match each of them to one of the different rape cases.

"This is like trying to put a jigsaw puzzle together without the picture on the box," Pete grumbled.

"We have twenty-two items and five rapes. Even if we had just five objects and five rapes, we wouldn't necessarily know which object was collected at which rape scene, since all the items are pretty generic. A rock could have come from any place." I was feeling Pete's frustration.

"Some of them probably come from earlier cases that we don't even know about," Pete admitted. "He didn't *just* start assaulting women."

We both knew that serial rapists, like serial murderers, have careers that start early in life. They begin with lesser crimes and move up to the big leagues. These objects could have represented a decade of assaults.

"And then when we're done, we're going to have to talk to the women again. I'm telling you, it's horrible. I should have taken the suspects. Whenever I talk to women who've been victimized, I think of my wife and girls." Pete was flipping through pictures of the crime scenes as he spoke. "The odds that they'll be assaulted are frighteningly high. And how the hell do you warn them without terrifying them?" he asked.

I thought it must be particularly hard for a cop to see all the dreadful harm that can befall people and then have to watch his children go out in that same world every day. I tried to change the subject.

"The rapes all occurred at different locations: the back of a van; behind a local bar; in a store restroom; another van; and in the bushes by the victim's house. We know that the souvenirs would have reminded him of the rapes, but did they come from the location of the rape, or maybe someplace close by? Hell, they might even have come from something else connected to the victim, like the first place he saw her." What had seemed like a great discovery was turning out to be a Rubik's Cube.

"That's why we're going to have to go back to the victims. Maybe they'll recognize one of the items, or maybe one of them will spark a memory," Pete said.

"All we have to do is prove that these objects," I tapped the photos we'd printed out, "even just one of them, are connected to the rapes, then we will have established Conway as the perp."

"And once we've done that we can focus on Nichols." Pete was about as even-tempered a man as I'd ever met, so what he said next surprised me. "I want to take him down."

"You sound like a movie cop," I told him.

"If we have a deputy who's dirty enough that he shot an innocent man, and possibly killed a woman to frame him, I take that very personally. Besides, we can't let your dad down."

It was funny. Pete always seemed like one of those guys for whom the job was just a job. He lived and breathed for his wife and girls. He almost never went out drinking with the guys, sat around telling war stories or collected sheriff patches. There were only two things about the work that he really seemed to enjoy—talking to people and shooting at the range. He'd told me once that he'd always thought he'd be a teacher when he was growing up. But now, in this moment, I realized how deeply he felt about the department.

"I'm going to start with this," I said, holding up a picture of the handicap parking sign. "If it was stolen from somewhere in Adams County within the last six months, I ought to be able to find out where. Plus, Marcus was able to pull fingerprints off of it."

"Makes sense." Pete nodded. "I'm going to start with the pen." He held up the picture of a Bic pen that read "Have a nice day!"

"Marcus got a partial off of it, and it's a bit distinctive. Also, I'll take this." Pete held up a picture of a screwdriver.

"How many should we tackle?" I added.

"Maybe we should work on all of them at once."

"What's the point in wasting time on a rock or a nail? They're too common. If we run into dead ends with these, we'll come back to them."

"And we won't talk to the victims until we have something we're confident is related to their case, or until we're at a dead end." His empathy for victims was one of the many reasons I liked being partnered with Pete.

"Agreed."

I heard my phone's text tone go off and looked down to see a message from Dad. *Meet me for lunch at the house.* I knew that he wanted a briefing on the autopsy and the search of Conway's house.

I'd no sooner confirmed that I'd meet Dad when another text came through. This one was from Eddie, my snitch. *Can you meet me at the usual place?* I just had time before heading over to Dad's.

CHAPTER EIGHTEEN

I drove to the back of Rose Hill Cemetery and parked next to *Caroline Thorne 1878 – 1918*. Eddie was sitting down, leaning against the cemetery's wall and waiting for me. Whenever he saw me, he looked like he was about to run. He stood up as I walked over to him and for a moment I thought he really would rabbit this time.

"You look more nervous than usual," I told him.

"I've got good reason. I want you to destroy everything with my name on it."

"What are you talking about?"

"If they find out about me, I'm dead. And they've got more than one deputy on the inside."

"You told me that from the beginning. What's changed?"

"They've killed someone. Before it was just drugs and women and stuff. But now I know they've killed someone, and not just a drug guy either. You got to destroy anything that might have my name on—"

I held up my hand to stop the words pouring out of his mouth. "Don't worry. I don't have a file with 'Eddie the Informer' written across the top."

"What about your phone?"

"I keep it with me all the time. Is this why you wanted to

meet?"

"Yes. No. I wanted you to know that my dad and all of them are going crazy. I've never seen them like this."

"Is that an angora sweater?" His jacket had blown open and I could just see something pink and fuzzy around his neckline.

"It's cashmere. And it makes me feel a little better, okay? I'm telling you, things aren't good!"

"Okay, slow down and tell me what you know."

"Dad's, like, gone into hiding. When I see him or any of the big guys, they're giving everyone this look. It's that look the Secret Service gives everyone. You know, like anyone could be guilty."

"That's fascinating," I said sarcastically, "but how does that help me?"

"I've heard things too. Dad's sure that your father is running some kind of sting on him."

"That's crazy. My dad's been after him for years. He's never made a secret of it. Besides, it doesn't even make sense. If your father has these moles in our department, wouldn't he know if we were running a special operation against him?"

"I think that's what's making him go berserk. He hasn't been too worried about your father's efforts in the past because he knew what was going on from the inside. But now he thinks your father is onto him and has found a way to target him without him knowing." Eddie was talking a mile a minute.

"I need you to give me the names of the deputies on the inside," I said, trying to get him to focus.

"I don't know who they are!" he yelled. "If I did, I'd tell you and get out of town. I thought I had a chance to find out, but now Dad's gone into, like, lockdown. I see him once in a while at the house. He eats and leaves."

"I thought you got on his good side when I helped you by taking out some of his competition."

"Yeah, but now he even finds that suspicious. For all I

know, he's using. Wouldn't that be a laugh? He asked me the other day why I'd suddenly got interested in the business. He knows I'm up to something. I saw it in his cold-ass eyes. Last time I saw him, Chief was trying to calm him down, but he wasn't having any of it."

"Chief?"

"My grandfather. We've always called him Chief," Eddie explained.

I'd met Daniel Thompson several times over the years while he was the fire chief in Calhoun. But unlike most first responders in the county, Dad never seemed on great terms with him. When I joined the department I learned why. As patriarch of the Thompson clan, Daniel managed to appear respectable as head of the fire department, but it was common knowledge that he oversaw the Thompson empire of drugs and other illicit activities in the county. But no one had ever even been able to charge Daniel Thompson with anything. Word was that he was a lot smarter than his son, Justin.

"Get me something I can use," I said, turning and walking away.

"Hey, I need—" Eddie started to say. He always hit me up for cash.

I turned around and started back toward him. "You need money? Well, I need information!" I was hot even as a cold wind blew out of the north, anger burning through me. "You'll get money when you tell me something I can use." I didn't wait for him to answer, but turned back around, got in my car and drove off.

My anger was fueled by fear and frustration. Eddie's nervous state had convinced me that there was trouble brewing with the Thompson clan. But why were they running so scared?

I drove straight to Dad's house. I found him walking the pasture with Mauser, who was enjoying the cool weather.

Dad had to call the big idiot a dozen times to get him to stop rolling in every disgusting thing he could find in the pasture.

Mauser was so enthralled with the smells that his humongous nose was picking up that he didn't notice me until he was headed for the gate. The big lummox almost knocked me down with his enthusiastic greeting.

"My God, dog, you stink!" I told him, trying to keep him from rubbing the smell off on me.

"Now you've done it. You need a bath," Dad said to Mauser, who looked not at all ashamed.

With my help, Dad managed to get Mauser into the crossties at the barn and hose him down. By the time we were done, Dad and I were as wet as the dog, but at least he smelled less like horse manure and more like oatmeal shampoo as we headed for the house.

Mauser was ready for his lunch. He stood back and let Dad set the bowl down in front of him before attacking the chow.

"Is Mauser all right?" I asked.

"What do you mean?"

"He let you put his lunch down without knocking the bowl out of your hand."

"That's Jamie's doing. He's been reinforcing Mauser's training."

"Jamie's the new kid you have walking him when you can't?"

"Yeah. He graduated last year and is going to Tallahassee Community College. You remember him. He was in the Sheriff's Explorers. Blond hair with a wannabe mustache and goatee?"

"Oh, yeah."

"In fact, he's still helping out with the Explorers."

"He's been training Mauser?" I was impressed.

"Reinforcing the training that I've done with him." Dad nodded his head.

I almost laughed out loud. Dad was the world's worst dog trainer. He wasn't bad with horses, but there was something about a dog that made him go soft. Dad's idea of training involved too many treats given at all the wrong times. But I didn't say anything, letting Dad believe his little myth. I felt a bit ashamed that I'd never followed through on my plans from a month ago to work with Mauser.

"So where are we?" Dad asked, done with the small talk.

I told him about the suitcase.

"I knew that Ayers wasn't our rapist. But Conway? Damn it!" Dad hit the table hard with his fist. "I should have seen it!"

"We don't have solid evidence yet that it was him. The stuff in the suitcase is just a bunch of junk until we tie some of it to the actual cases."

Dad held up his hand. "I know. But I'm comfortable going under the assumption that Ayers was innocent of the first five rapes, and therefore is unlikely to have attacked Angie Maitland."

"Agreed. Which leaves us with Nichols. I saw Matt talking to Nichols away from the office yesterday."

"Crap. I keep hoping against hope that he's clean. I know that he's not well liked, but he's always seemed dedicated to the job. But unfortunately, I've got something too." Dad opened his laptop and pulled up a map. "Here's the tracking data on Matt's car for Wednesday. He was at the Sweet Spot again. Stayed parked there from eleven until four in the morning."

"You figure he hooked up with someone there?" I asked.

"Maybe. They would have had enough time to help Nichols and then take care of Conway."

"And you think they killed Conway so that there wouldn't be any more rapes?" I was trying to see all the angles.

"That's right. If they were going to use the rapes as a way to embarrass me, then they had to make sure they ended with the death of Ayers."

"This sounds a bit convoluted. Justin Thompson's a lot of things, but no one has ever accused him of playing eleventh-dimensional chess." I couldn't quite see it. But then I remembered what Eddie had told me. "Of course, my snitch just told me that Justin is all worked up. Utterly convinced that you're after him."

"I *am* after him."

"Yeah, but after him in some back-door way. Like something that you're keeping close to your vest so that his moles can't keep track of it."

"How could I do that? Our vice squad consists of one full-time investigator and four deputies who work as needed. Sure, I've got a file on most of the Thompsons. All the bad ones." There was a branch of the family that had disavowed the criminal half. "We arrest them when we can, and I've tried to get FDLE involved, but on a state level our bad guys are pretty low rent. Maybe they've started using their own product. That would explain the paranoia."

"Maybe."

"I'm more concerned with Nichols and Matt."

"I think Pete and I are close to being able to move on Nichols. At least we're close to putting some real pressure on him."

"Eliminating Ayers as a suspect in the rapes helps, but you still have to tie Nichols to the woman's murder, or be able to come up with a convincing motive. Maybe it was to embarrass me, but even *you're* skeptical of that. The State Attorney is going to want something more substantial before he goes in front of a jury."

"First, we tie Conway to the rapes and then we look at Nichols for the murders of Maitland, Ayers and Conway. If we can put enough pressure on Nichols while offering him some small concession on the charges, he'll probably finger everyone else," I said.

"Including Matt?"

"Maybe," I said, then stopped and really looked at Dad. His uniform seemed to sag on him. *Has he lost weight?* He looked tired.

"You know, you don't have to run for sheriff again." I

117

wanted him to know that he didn't owe anyone anything. He'd served this community well for many years, and I didn't want to see it tear him down like this. But from the way he reacted, you would have thought I'd suggested he surrender to ISIS. He stood up straight and looked me square in the eyes.

"I am not being run off! I'll see this through no matter where it leads. If it's too hot for you… Well, I'll understand. And if it means I lose the election, so be it. But I am *not* quitting."

"That's not what I meant. You just look exhausted."

"I've been tired before." He waved it off. "That's not going to slow me down."

It was clear that I'd pissed him off, but I was worried about him. It was a habit I got into after Mom died. These days, though, trying to protect the people I cared about was just getting me in trouble.

CHAPTER NINETEEN

After curt goodbyes, we both went back to work. I headed down to the county's public works department in search of information on Conway's metal sign.

Public works consisted of six buildings spread over a dozen acres on the edge of town. I'd dealt with them regularly when I was on patrol. Not a week went by that I hadn't needed to get ahold of them to repair a pot hole, cut up a tree or replace a road sign, but since I'd become an investigator I'd lost touch with who was running the show. Public works seemed to be a constant bone of contention with the powers that be. If there wasn't an uproar over the lack of response by the department, then there was a corruption scandal shaking the place up. I remembered hearing last fall about one of the county commissioners using the department to fix their driveway. Doesn't anyone ever learn?

I hunted up one of the old timers that I'd made friends with years ago, someone who could be counted on to have the low-down on the department. I found Freddy sitting behind a desk in a building marked "Hazardous Waste Disposal."

"Hey, Freddy, how's it going?" I said loudly, causing the

older man to look up from a catalog of machines and parts.

"Hey, hey, if it ain't Deputy Dog," he said good-naturedly. He gave me a huge smile while wiping sweat from his bald head. No matter how cold it was, I'd never seen him when he wasn't sweating. "Betcha need a favor."

"How'd you know?"

"Somebody I ain't seen in a year shows up, I know they want somethin'." His Boston accent made him unique in Adams County. I was pretty sure that no one else in the county sounded like him, and I knew he enjoyed playing it up.

I showed him the picture of the parking fine sign. "Who's in charge of replacing signs these days?"

"Chad runs the sign shop. But Misty takes the requests and does the billing and stuff. And don't get excited. She's not half as good lookin' as the name would imply," he said, shaking his head sadly.

"She's over in the main office?" I asked, ignoring his sexism.

"Yeah. Hey, I got a nephew who wants to be a cop. Crazy. Why would anyone want to be sticking their noses in other peoples' trouble all the time? That's what I told him."

"You're a wise man, Freddy," I said, turning to go.

"Yeah, come back next time you need anything," he said with a laugh.

"I pay my debts. Call me if I can help you out."

"I'll take you up on that someday," he answered, looking back at his catalog.

I found Misty in her own office tucked away in the main building. Her desk was piled high with neat stacks of invoices and purchase orders.

"Can I help you?" she asked pertly, looking up from a large computer monitor. In her late fifties, she was apparently trying to make up for her wrinkles by adding perfume.

"I hope so," I said, trying not to gag. I showed her the picture of the sign. "Have you all replaced one of these in the last three months?"

"Handicap five-hundred-dollar parking fine sign," she said, turning back to her screen and clicking keys with one hand while making rhythmic motions with a mouse. "Yes, we have," she said, sounding a little surprised.

I waited, but she didn't add anything.

"Where?"

"Where what? Oh, where was the sign. Why didn't you ask that? 2345 Oak Street North. It's the Calhoun Place strip mall."

"Does it say which sign?" I knew there were a dozen handicap spots in the parking lot.

"No. Why don't you ask your guy?" she said. "Deputy Nichols reported it."

I felt my stomach drop to my knees. "Really?" was all I could think to say for a minute. "When did he report it?"

"January fourth." Misty looked bored. "I've really got a lot of work to do."

I called Pete as I left public works. "The sign is from Calhoun Place where the third victim was raped. It was reported missing on January fourth, but here's the kicker. Nichols was the officer who reported it missing."

"Nichols, that's interesting. I'm not sure that it means too much, though," Pete mused.

"Raises the question of when he knew Conway was the rapist."

"Did he know that Conway had taken the sign and was replacing it to cover it up?"

"Could Nichols have been involved in the rapes from the beginning?"

"Possibly, but none of the victims mentioned a second person. I showed Linda Evers photos of all the items from the suitcase. She thought the pen might have come from her van." He paused a minute, then said, "I really want to pull Nichols in and put his feet to the fire."

"We do that, he's going to either clam up or go postal."

"Yeah, and we probably need to talk to the lieutenant

before we do it."

"And Major Parks. Don't forget he's supposed to be heading up the internal affairs review of the shooting," I reminded Pete.

"Jeez, could this be any more complicated? But you're right. Once we let Nichols know that we suspect him, it can't be undone."

"Nichols will stir up a shit storm inside the department and will make himself the victim of the story. All that said, I still want to do it."

"Since when did you become such a gambler?"

"Risk-taking is my game."

"Yeah, right, I'm not buying that. Okay, let's talk to Lt. Johnson and Major Parks this afternoon so our asses are well covered."

"Deal."

"I don't like any of this," Lt. Johnson said, staring back and forth between Pete and me. We'd spent twenty minutes giving him and Parks the abbreviated version of our investigation. Now we had to wait to see which side of the equation they were going to come down on: caution or action. Johnson telegraphed his military background with every move he made. He was always dressed in uniform and sat, stood and walked like was he being graded on posture. And no man, not even my father, could glare someone down better than Lt. Johnson.

"We'd have brought you all in sooner, but the investigation has been moving fast," Pete explained.

"Accusing one of our deputies of murder is as serious as it gets." Major Parks stated the obvious.

"The sooner we put him under the lights, the quicker we can settle this." I knew this was the only golden ring that I could offer them. Everyone would want this to be over as quickly as possible. Of course, I wasn't going to tell either of them that this was probably part of a larger conspiracy. Even

Pete didn't know all of the angles, which bothered me a lot more than keeping the brass in the dark.

"I'm not stupid. I know what you're doing. Like a chemical reaction, you think if you add heat it'll speed things up. Trouble is, sometimes when you add heat, things blow up." Johnson was glaring at us again.

I tried to meet his eyes without making it a challenge and kept my mouth shut so he didn't think I was rushing him into a decision.

"Hmmm. I think I've got a job for you." Johnson pointed his finger at me in a very nice impression of Uncle Sam. "Okay, you two can interview Nichols, put some heat on him and see where it goes. But we'll be watching, and I'll pull the plug if I think for one moment you're going too far." He turned to the major. "Is that acceptable, Major?"

"If there's a bad egg in the department, we need to find out as soon as possible," Parks said, nodding.

"What's the job you have for me?" I asked Johnson.

"Regardless of what happens with the Nichols interview, I want you to take one morning in the next day or so to help Greene clear a couple of his cases. He's been taking most of the new stuff while you two have been tied up with this shooting."

His tone left no doubt that this was an order and not a real trade that I could negotiate. He wasn't going to make Pete do it considering the well-known bad blood between Pete and Matt. But the thought of having to work with Matt right now made my blood run cold. What choice did I have?

"Okay." At least we were going to have our chance to bring the hammer down on Nichols. Maybe Nichols would crumble and implicate Matt and I wouldn't have to deal with him tomorrow. Fat chance. We'd be lucky if Nichols implicated himself. But it was worth the chance.

It was four by the time we got out of Johnson's office. "I'll call Nichols and see if he can come in at five. That'd give us an hour to prepare," Pete said.

"Are we jumping the gun on this?" I asked, suddenly

experiencing a bad case of cold feet.

"We can do this. Even if we don't hit gold this afternoon, we're going to push Nichols hard enough that he's going to get desperate. Desperate men do dumb shit. I think Confucius or that guy who wrote the *Art of War* said that."

"Okay, make the call."

I gathered from Pete's side of the phone call that Nichols was suspicious.

"It's just routine. We want to clear up one or two more points. You know Parks and Johnson can be asses about the details," Pete told Nichols. I didn't hear his response, but Pete smiled.

"Yep, see you then." Pete hung up and turned to me. "Let's go."

CHAPTER TWENTY

We made our final plans in the conference room. Like before, we wanted Nichols to think the meeting was informal. I glanced up at the camera mounted high up in the corner of the room. Similar to the ones used in our regular interview rooms, the camera would allow Johnson, Parks and my dad to watch the interview as it took place.

"We'll tell the desk sergeant to let Nichols come straight back here," Pete said.

"Right, no escort, everything low-key. And we'll be sitting here with the file on the shooting." I tapped the four-inch-high pile of notes, reports and photographs. "Which he'll be very curious about."

"Exactly. It'll distract him so that he's paying less attention to our questions and his answers. Which is also the purpose of having these on our side of the table." Pete pulled out Nichols's gun and badge, laying them next to us on the table. "Major Parks was reluctant to hand them over. He made me assure him that I wouldn't give them back to Nichols under any circumstances."

"I'm not surprised. It doesn't matter. Everyone in the office will know that we're pointing the finger at Nichols half an hour after we're done," I said regretfully. The sheriff's office was a very small family.

"You know, we won't be very popular until we prove he's guilty."

I knew Pete was understating the case. This was going to create a large rift in the family. Nichols was not one of the most popular deputies, but he had friends. And many wouldn't believe he was guilty even with proof. Once people have made up their minds about someone, it can be hard to get them to change their opinion.

"I can live with not being popular," I said lightly.

"Hell, you aren't that popular anyway," Pete joked, lightening the mood a bit. "Who starts asking the questions?"

"You. He'll see you as the senior investigator. Start easy, get tough, that's our motto."

"I'll even suggest that he could walk out with his badge and gun," Pete said, tapping them. "You know he'll probably be armed."

"Probably? Guaranteed. And that's the risk we're taking going with the casual interview scheme. We can change our minds and treat him like we would any suspect, including a search before we bring him in. But I say we take our chances."

Pete agreed, but we both found ourselves unconsciously adjusting our posture and our handguns so that they would be easily accessible. I hated to admit it, but I was depending on Pete getting the draw on Nichols if things went south. I was pretty good, but Pete was the man when it came to the quick draw.

Nichols walked in fifteen minutes later. Pete and I pretended to be absorbed in the case file. We looked up casually and greeted him. Nichols was dressed in a polo shirt and jeans and looked relaxed.

"That the file?" he asked, trying to glance at it from the opposite side of the table.

"Yeah, we've almost got everything we need," Pete said. "Have a seat. We've just got a couple more i's to cross and t's to dot," he joked. "We need to get you back on duty." He nodded to the gun and shield sitting on our side of the table.

"I hear that," Nichols said, seating himself across from us. I noticed that he didn't pull his chair in all the way to the table. Better access to his concealed gun?

"We got your report and, with our earlier interview, we have a clear picture of your account of the shooting. However, a few discrepancies have come up."

Pete shuffled through the papers. I noticed Nichols looking at his gun and shield longingly.

"Here's one of our problems," Pete said, looking at a report of my interview with the neighborhood watch professional, Mrs. Gavin. "We have a witness who states that you pulled up behind the shopping center and turned off your lights for a few minutes, then turned them back on about the time she reports hearing the shots." Pete paused as though he was trying to figure something out. "See, that doesn't fit with your account at all."

"Witness?" Nichols asked in a cold and brittle tone. But he didn't sound too surprised. I thought that was odd.

"Yeah," Pete said, not elaborating and just letting Nichols stew on it.

"I gave you my account. That's the way it happened." Nichols had tensed up and his friendly tone was completely gone.

"Of course," Pete said lightly. "We just have this witness…" He let that hang, implying that we wanted to dismiss the witness as much as Nichols wanted us to.

"Well, I don't know what to tell you. I can't change my story to fit your witness." He had relaxed a little, but was still clearly on guard. "Who's this witness? Where was she?"

Pete had a decision to make. Should he give a little information in order to get the interview back on track? "Just some old busybody. But if we can get that cleared up, it will make it a lot easier to move forward." Pete glanced again at the gun and badge sitting on the table next to him. Nichols's eyes followed Pete's.

"I see that. You know, now that I think back on it, I might have turned my lights off." *Got him*, I thought. Nothing says "guilty" like changing your story when confronted with facts.

"I came around the building looking for anything out of place, like I told you. Now that I remember, I turned my lights off so that I wouldn't scare off anyone who was doing something they shouldn't. You know, breaking-in or engaging in an illicit act."

"Makes sense. You were trying to catch them with their pants down," Pete said lightly and smiling.

I could see Nichols relaxing again, and I got ready for my big scene. Pete and I had practiced this several times.

"Okay. That pretty much clears everything up," Pete said, putting papers back in the file. Once he had everything gathered up, he reached over and put his hand on Nichols's gun and badge and began to slide them across the table to Nichols.

"Wait, there was that one other little thing," I said on cue, reaching out and pulling a photo from underneath the file. Nichols glanced over at me, but his eyes went back to his gun and shield, so close and yet still out of reach.

I held up the photo of the handicap sign. "Did you report this as missing?"

As Nichols looked at the picture it felt like someone had opened the window and let the icy cold January wind blow through the room. His mouth dropped open and his eyes betrayed him. He knew the significance of us having that sign. His brain couldn't switch gears fast enough.

"I... I might have. I think I did report a sign like that missing." But he realized he'd taken too long to come up with the answer. "What does that have to do with the shooting?" His voice was cold and defensive.

Pete slid the gun and badge back to our side of the table. Nichols's right hand left the table and went out of sight. At the same time, Pete's hand went down to his waist and he smiled at Nichols.

"It has to do with the rapes. Would you like to tell us the real story now?" Pete asked calmly.

Nichols thought long and hard about his next move. Finally he said, "I think you're just screwing with me." He stood up. "I think I'll bring my lawyer the next time you all want to chat." He waited for us to respond, but we just stared back at him. He slammed the door when he left.

My one regret from the interview was that I couldn't ask Nichols about his meeting with Matt.

Dad walked into the room as we were gathering up the file. "Okay, you proved it to us," he said. "Now you just have to get some solid evidence on him."

"I've been thinking about that," I said. "I'm going to take Shantel back to the Conway house and go over everything again. If we can find a fingerprint or any other evidence that Nichols was in the house, or by the pool, we'd be a lot closer to having something we can take to court."

By the time I got home, Ivy was mad at me for a late dinner and for not giving her a full evening of cuddle time. I tried to buy her off with some turkey from the sandwich I'd picked up for dinner. She forgave me enough to choke down her turkey.

I texted Cara: *Just got home. Call if you have the time.* My phone rang a couple minutes later.

"Long day?" she asked, which just felt awkward.

"At least I feel like we're making progress on the case. How about you?"

"Normal day at the farm." The farm was her nickname for work, sort of a pun on the vet's name. "Dr. Barnhill had offered to do several free spays and neuters for the shelter, which is great of him, but he hadn't let Sandra know so the schedule was totally screwed. I didn't get home much earlier than you."

"Would you like to do something together this weekend?" I knew I was pushing things, but couldn't stop myself.

There was a long pause. "Maybe. Call me Thursday." She wasn't as quick to forgive as Ivy. I couldn't decide if she was really considering it or was simply putting off telling me no.

We talked for a few more minutes and I rashly ended the call with, "I love you."

"I love you too," she said, but it was shrouded in such a tone of sadness that it didn't give me much hope.

CHAPTER TWENTY-ONE

I got to the office early on Tuesday. Not my favorite thing to do on a cold and frosty winter morning. A dozen times each winter there was enough ice on the windshield that I had to use the plastic scraper I kept in the trunk. This was one of those mornings. But Shantel had told me to get there before eight if I wanted to cart her off to the Conway house.

"If you give them a chance, they're going to find something else for me to do. We get gone before anyone else gets there, and I can spend most of the day helping you go over your crime scene," she'd told me.

For me, going off with Shantel meant I had a good excuse to put off working with Matt. So I was there to greet her as soon as she walked in the door. I helped her gather up some supplies and equipment and off we went.

"So what has you looking like a boy who's lost his puppy?" Shantel asked after she had me stop and buy her a coffee.

"I don't know what you're talking about." I did, but I wasn't in the mood to get into it, especially not before nine in the morning.

"Still having problems with your girl?"

"I really don't want to talk about it," I said, giving her the eye.

"Well, that's too bad. 'Cause I don't intend on working all day with your old mopey face. So get a damn smile going or tell me what the problem is."

"I just bought you a cup of coffee and you talk to me that way?" I asked, trying desperately to redirect her attention.

"You bought me this coffee because I'm going out to your crime scene to crawl around on my hands and knees looking for the smoking gun that might pull you out of the cesspool that you and Pete find yourselves in. Now you tell Aunt Shantel what's got you looking like the Internet's next grumpy candidate. I already know it's the girl. So come on and spill your guts before we get to the crime scene so we aren't wasting time."

"You're right. It's the girl." I thought if I admitted it quickly, I could cut this off sooner rather than later.

"Details. Come on. I'm a woman. Maybe I can help. Bound to make you feel better talking about it. 'Sides, we'll get it out of the way early."

I looked at her. Why the hell didn't we have her doing interrogations?

"Fine. She's pissed at me because I didn't fill her in on all the gory details when we found Conway's body."

"Uh, huh."

I didn't look, but I was sure Shantel was shaking her head sadly.

"What?" I asked, exasperated.

She just kept shaking her head. Knowing that it wasn't going to end there, I sighed heavily.

"Is it unreasonable to want to keep the crap in my life separate for the things that are good?" I really didn't want to have this argument with Shantel. As much as I respected her and appreciated her friendship, I'd always thought that she didn't have a reasonable sense of where other's personal space began.

"I got my thoughts on that," she said and then added, "If you want to hear them."

I'm sure you do, I thought. What choice did I have?

"Well…" I hesitated. We weren't that far from the Conway house.

"You're damn lucky," she said bluntly.

"I don't quite follow." I wasn't liking where this was going.

"You know I was married?"

"Yeahhhh." I vaguely remembered her mentioning it.

"He was in the Army. A Ranger out of Fort Hood. We got married—I was twenty-two, he was twenty-five. His name's DeWayne. Second year we were married, he got sent overseas. Middle East. We were able to talk to each other once in a while. Neither of us were big letter writers. I thought we were getting along fine. I missed him. Still loved him. I'd gone home to live with my family and finished school."

Where is this going? I wondered in my I-still-haven't-completely-woken-up-yet state.

"We're almost there." I turned onto the drive that led to Conway's house.

"Yeah, well, you can just park it and listen to me." Shantel knew I was trying to get out of her lecture. "As I was saying, I worried about him getting hurt. But I never thought about what he was going through. I mean inside. When DeWayne came home nine months later, I was all about making him happy and getting our lives on a path to having a home and maybe, God willing, some kids. But, and here's the thing, I was all wrapped up in my world, my life that I thought was his world too. But it wasn't, or at least not all of it. And right then it wasn't the part of his life that was most important to him."

I parked the car in front of the locked gate and turned to look at Shantel. She took a drink from her cup of coffee, steam still rising off the top.

"Before I knew it, we weren't a couple anymore. He was in his world and I was in mine. I should have cared more. He tried to be as concerned with all the details of our life as I was, but both of us were missing the point." She stopped and stared at me.

"And what was the point?" I asked, knowing that was the quickest route to getting to wherever we were going.

"What was over there…" Shantel waved a mocha-colored hand vaguely toward the east, "…in that desert, was a part of him, a part of us. As the months went by he got mad. We had fights. I got madder. Crazy shit. Finally, we both knew it was over."

The emotion in her voice was beginning to break down my irritation. But I still didn't really see her point.

"What you're saying seems to agree with me. Living a life that's full of crap destroys the good in life. My point is to keep the one from infecting the other," I argued.

"No, you're wrong. DeWayne got remarried about six months after we separated. A girl from our neighborhood back in Savannah. Funny… Growing up she was all tomboy. Never hung out much with the girls. Pretty, but nothing compared to me." Shantel smiled. "Her name's Theresa. She'd gone to work for her dad's trucking company. She's running it now. DeWayne stayed in the Army, had more deployments.

"I saw them about ten years after they were married. Both of them seemed really happy, and I was glad for them. Five years earlier and I might have torn her hair out, but I'd gotten over it in a decade. One night I got the chance to talk to them, and I asked how they dealt with DeWayne being overseas and all the problems that went along with it." Shantel paused for dramatic effect.

"And?" Against my better judgment I kind of wanted to know. I respected Shantel's no-nonsense attitude.

"DeWayne spoke first. He said that she asked him about everything. Wanted to know all the details that went on when he was in a war zone. Sometimes there would be stuff that he didn't want to tell her, or that he hadn't had time to process, but eventually he'd tell her because he knew she really wanted to be a part of his life. *Every* part of his life. My mistake was being in love with the man I wanted DeWayne to be and the life that I wanted for us. Theresa was in love with the *real* DeWayne, and she wanted to be a part of his life no matter what that life involved. And DeWayne needed someone to share the bad experiences with more than he needed a wife to share the good times. Theresa knew that. Sounds like Cara knows it too."

Shantel let that hang in the air for a bit, giving me a stern look. Then she threw open her door to the cold morning air and said, "Let's go find some evidence. Oh, that reminds me. Our IT guy said that the phone from the hot tub was a burner that hadn't even been used yet. So no luck there, and he added that if you ever send him something that smells that bad again, he'll make sure you can never log on to another computer as long as you live."

"There are days that wouldn't break my heart," I said honestly.

Shantel got out and opened the lock on the gate and I drove the car up to the house, thinking about what she had said.

The big house, surrounded by woods in the frosty morning light, looked like a monument to a dead world. Which is what it had become for the Conways. A reminder of a life when they had a child, a boy that represented their hopes and dreams for the future. Now it would be a memorial to a future that could never be.

I was carrying most of the equipment, so Shantel opened the door. We got to work combing the house for fingerprints and trace evidence. By noon we'd vacuumed most of the house and dusted the doorknobs, appliances and countertops. After a lunch break we tackled the bathrooms, delving into the drains to pull out hair and other unsavory items.

Exhausted, I told Shantel, "Enough."

"You're right about that," she said, indicating the three boxes of trace evidence we'd collected. "All of this and we'll be lucky if we got one hair or a latent fingerprint that matches Nichols."

"That's all we need. He's never officially been here, and he claimed that he'd never been here for any other reason, so if we can find something that proves he was in the house, we'll have caught him lying about being at a crime scene. A crime scene linked to a shooting that he was involved in."

"He always seemed like one of the good ones," Shantel said thoughtfully. I knew what she meant.

"That's life. How often do you get the outcome you expected or wanted?" I picked up one of the boxes and headed for the door.

After dropping Shantel and the evidence at the office, I drove home, thinking about the advice she'd given me. As soon as I walked in the door, I called Cara.

"I've been thinking about what you said," I started out weakly.

"Like what?" She said it a bit tauntingly, but it sounded like she was in a good mood. I was encouraged.

"Look, I don't want to talk over the phone. Can I come over? Or could we meet someplace?" There was a long pause as she thought this over. I figured I should put her mind at ease. "If you're afraid that we might get into an argument, you have nothing to worry about. I'm prepared to surrender unconditionally."

"Seriously?" She sounded perplexed.

"Listen, I'll tell you all about it when I see you." I left it open for her to decide when that would be.

"Hot chocolate at my place?" she suggested tentatively.

"That sounds great to me," I answered sincerely.

Ten minutes later, having explained to Ivy that I wasn't going to be able to spend all evening scratching her belly and receiving a disapproving look in return from the strong-minded tabby, I was out the door and headed back to town.

I knocked on the door and waited under the porch light, watching my breath in the night air. When Cara opened the door, my heart swelled at the sight of her and any misgivings I had about capitulating melted away.

"You said that you were surrendering. I didn't really see this as a war," she said earnestly as we sipped our hot chocolate on the couch.

"I was kind of kidding. I just meant that, having thought about things, I can see your point of view." I didn't tell her about Shantel's input. I didn't want to complicate the discussion.

"You understand that I want to be a part of your life?"

"Yes, all of my life. I think I get it. And I want to be a part of yours. I want to know what upsets you or worries you or, hell, just pisses you off."

"Exactly." She leaned over and kissed me lightly. "I know your job sucks sometimes and it's dangerous. But I want to be there for you, and to do that I have to know what you're going through." Cara set down her mug and leaned into me, hugging my arm. Alvin, who was curled up on the other side of Cara, let out a little huff as he readjusted himself.

"It makes sense. But you have to know that there will be times when I have to process events in my own head before I can tell you about them."

"I know, and maybe that's where I was wrong. Pressing you too hard. But if you promise me that you won't hold things back, that you'll tell me what you can when you can... Well," Cara pulled my head around and kissed me passionately, "maybe I can find a way to make you feel better. That's all I want."

"A kiss won't heal all wounds."

"A kiss never made things worse," she told me and we dislodged Alvin from his place on the couch.

When I looked at my watch it was past midnight. "I've got to go," I said, putting my shirt back on and looking for my shoes.

"You can stay here."

"I've got to get up early tomorrow." I cringed when I thought about my bargain with Lt. Johnson. I couldn't put off working with Matt any longer. The thought of spending most of the day with Matt, who I'd never been fond of and now suspected of colluding with men who were determined to damage my father and the department, made me sick to my stomach.

I remembered my promise to Cara and explained, "I've got to work with Matt tomorrow and I'm not looking forward to it. I haven't told you everything about him, some of it I can't. I'll tell you all I can later." I stopped putting on my shoe and looked at her. "I should be able to have one day off this weekend. Can we go somewhere?"

"I'd like that."

CHAPTER TWENTY-TWO

Morning came early. My first thought was that I needed to hurry and get into work. Then I remembered what my day was probably going to be like and my second thought was: *To hell with hurrying!* I spent forty-five minutes longer than I should have eating my cornflakes and giving Ivy some attention before heading to the office.

"Lt. Johnson thought you needed some help with your case load." This was the least confrontational statement I had been able to think of on my way to Matt's desk.

He looked up at me with hooded eyes. "The lieutenant said I'd get some help." His look implied that he wasn't happy with the help he was getting.

"I thought you were a type-A personality. I'm surprised you need help." I couldn't resist the chance to give the smug bastard a hard time.

"I've been carrying your and your lazy partner's cases for the last week."

"You might have heard that one of our deputies was involved in a shooting. I'm sorry if everyone has to step up and carry a little bit of the weight while we look into it." I knew I was taking this too far, but I couldn't help myself. Ever since I began to suspect him, I'd tried to avoid contact

139

for this very reason. My impulse control wasn't always what it should have been.

"I heard. Maybe your father should look beyond his own family when assigning important cases."

I felt my blood rise, but before I could open my mouth, Matt raised a hand to stop me.

"I'm sorry," he said with something approaching sincerity. I almost got whiplash from his change of direction. I'm sure my mouth fell open.

"Look, I've just been working hard. I really would appreciate your help on a couple of these." He indicated the pile of case folders on his desk.

Now I knew he was into something crooked. The Matt I knew never would have poured water on one of our fights. He didn't want trouble because he didn't want too much scrutiny. Fine. I'd take the opportunity to try and catch him out. I was pretty sure that he didn't know I suspected him of anything. Honestly, I didn't care if he did.

"Here are a domestic and a burglary. Both of them need some follow-up." He held out the folders.

I thought about making some smartass comment, but decided the best thing I could do was keep my mouth shut. I took the folders and sat down at my desk.

An hour later I walked back over to Matt. "How'd it go?" he asked, all sunshine and rainbows.

"The burglary I was able to link to two others. Deputy Ortiz is working on those and said that he'd go over it and see if it fits the MO of the others. If it does, he'll ask Lt. Johnson to let him have it. The perp in the domestic is going to plead guilty to a lesser charge. I talked with the State Attorney and he agreed as long as the husband agrees to pay the hospital bills as restitution. There was also a restraining order thrown in for good measure. I wrote up the reports. They're in the online files."

"Great. Look, there's one other I want your opinion on."

"What is it?"

"A shooting," he said, looking me hard in the eyes.

"Sure. What happened?" I asked warily.

"A black male was shot standing on the corner of Jefferson and Alabama in the late hours a couple Saturdays ago."

"I remember that."

"I was on call and got out there by five Sunday morning."

"Drugs?"

"No doubt. But, and it's a big but, one of my witnesses said that he saw a car at the time of the shooting. Didn't actually see the car *at* the shooting because he was a block away. However, he's sure that the car must have been there."

"I don't get it. You have a car at the scene or at least close to the scene. That's good, right?"

"My witness is a three-time loser who knows every cop and deputy in the county. He's sure that the person driving the car was a deputy," Matt said, looking me straight in the eyes, the same way you try and intimidate a suspect.

"So who did he think was driving the car?" I had no idea where this was going.

"There's the rub. He doesn't know. He just knows that he saw a cop. He was high at the time. He's always high and doesn't remember who it was, even if he knew at the time. Dud's his name. He just knows that his cop radar went off when he saw the driver."

"Dud? Seriously, he's having a good day when he's not actually in a drug-induced coma. Can he even see more than ten feet in front of what's left of his face?" I couldn't believe that Matt was giving Dud any credibility as a witness. "Is there any other evidence?"

"No."

"That's it?" Matt must have been going crazy trying to maintain a double life. None of this made any sense. "Do you have any other witnesses?"

"None that saw the murder or think they saw the killer. Just Dud." Matt continued to look at me as though searching for some answer that I was sure I didn't have.

"The autopsy didn't reveal anything?"

"No, just that one of the nine-millimeter bullets passed through the victim's chest and the other through his head. The second one killed him. From the angle that the bullets entered the victim, it looks like the killer stayed in his car."

"Motive?"

"Martin Thomas owed a lot of people money and was heavily into heroin. It's not a big stretch to think that he owed his drug connection money, or that he'd stolen money or drugs from the wrong person. Certainly no one tried to rob him since it would have been obvious to anyone that he was broke. And Mr. Thomas didn't have any life other than drugs at that point, so all the love angle motives are non-starters."

"So it could have just been drug-related?"

"Possibly."

I didn't know what to say at that point. Matt was confusing the hell out of me. Why bring up the possibility of a cop being involved? It didn't make sense.

"So how can I help?" I asked. The whole conversation felt surreal.

"If there was a bad deputy in the department, who do you think it could be?" Matt asked flatly.

Now I knew he was playing with me. "I can't imagine," I said.

"Hard to envision, isn't it?"

We stared at each other for another moment. Then I realized that I should treat him like a suspect. When you're interrogating a suspect you try to understand him, or at least try to make him *believe* that you're trying to understand him. You sympathize. On TV you always see the cops yelling, screaming and threatening the suspect, but it doesn't happen that way. Maybe a little tough talk, but honey does catch more flies than vinegar.

"Matt, I know we don't always see eye to eye, but we do work together. We even have to depend on each other. Let me take you to lunch. We can talk more about this then." I said it like a friend would to another friend. I even managed a smile. I just had to see him as a suspect, someone to be tricked.

"Okay." He smiled back at me. "Maybe I've been a bit unfair to you."

"That's the ticket. Winston's Grill okay?"

"That'll work."

Once we were seated and placed our order, I had time to think about how best to get some useful information out of Matt. I realized I didn't know much about him. He wasn't the type to hang out with the other guys. Come to think of it, neither was I.

"I just realized I don't really know much about you."

"Wow, this is like our first date," he shot back. If I liked him better, his sarcasm would have been funny.

"Just trying to be... frenemies?" I shrugged.

"I could throw it back to you. I know that your father's the sheriff and that, when you want to be, you're not a bad investigator. But beyond that..." He shrugged.

"There's not much to know. I grew up here in Adams County. Dad was a deputy for as far back as I can remember and then, when my mom died, Dad ran for sheriff and won. I joined the department because he asked me to."

"That's odd. You became a deputy just because your dad asked you to?" He smirked.

"It's a bit more complicated than that. I wanted Dad to run for sheriff to jog him out of the depression he'd fallen into after Mom died. We kind of made a deal. He runs and, if he wins, I join the department."

"Still seems a bit strange."

"I guess we were both trying to help each other out. I thought he needed a reason for moving on with his life, and he thought I needed to focus on a career. Being a deputy had been a good life for him. I guess he thought it would be a good life for me."

"And has it been?" Matt asked, almost sounding like he

143

gave a damn.

"Jury is still out on that one. There's good and bad. I don't think it's what I would have picked for myself." *How did I lose control of this conversation?* I asked myself. I needed to take charge. "What about you? Why'd you become a deputy, and how the hell did you end up here?" I tried to make it sound light-hearted.

"Good questions. I grew up in Orlando and I wanted to be a doctor. Or thought I did. I got through pre-med and then got into medical school down in Gainesville. But once I got in, I didn't like the way doctors become slaves to the system. You'd think that they'd be the gods of the hospital, but in reality it's the lawyers and the bean counters. So I dropped out and went to work as an EMT."

"EMT to cop isn't too much of a leap." I'd heard similar stories from more than one law enforcement officer.

"Got tired of being the guy cleaning up the mess and thought maybe I could be the one who stops it from happening in the first place. Went to work for the Jacksonville Police Department. Got married for a while, but that didn't work out so well."

That was a bit of an understatement. Everyone knew that Matt's ex-wife had tried to commit suicide, then moved across country to California. Life with Matt may not have been the cause of her problems, but I doubt it helped.

"So why here?"

"I got accepted to grad school at Florida State, so I needed to find something closer to FSU. I knew Chief Maxwell from high school and contacted him. He didn't have any openings on the police force at the time, but the sheriff's department did. So I was able to work here while getting my master's in criminology."

"So it's just a matter of time before you move on. FBI, DEA, ATF?"

"Everyone here knows I've been putting in my applications for the last couple of years. And I've made it through most of the interview process with the FBI and the

DEA. No luck with the ATF or the U.S. Marshals. Like you said, though, it's just a matter of time."

"You don't really like us much, do you?"

"Who? You? Your father? The department? The county?"

"Any of it."

"It's been an okay place to do what I needed to do. But I'm ready to move on. I don't think the Adams County Sheriff's Office has done much to sweeten my CV or to make me a better law enforcement officer."

"Maybe you haven't given it a chance. My dad's a damn good sheriff."

"He hasn't given me much of a chance. I've been doing mostly grunt work since I started."

"Are you kidding me? You became an investigator quicker than any deputy other than—" I broke off, knowing where this was going.

"Yeah, other than you. He moved his own son off the street faster than me. You hadn't put in your time. This place is full of nepotism and good ol' boy handouts. That oaf you call a partner would have been fired from any real department for what he did, stuffing his face with his radio turned down while I was running for my life." Matt spat the words out. The contempt that he had for us finally came shining through.

"Pete was punished, and he's a damn fine investigator. He was kept on because he's an asset to the department and my father knows it. Pete made a mistake. It wasn't out of malice or incompetence. All of us have made foolish mistakes. We're human."

"That would have been some comfort to me if I'd been killed that night. Knowing that you are all just human, and you make mistakes. What about you? You aren't a complete waste. Why don't you go somewhere where your father won't overshadow your accomplishments?"

The words stung, but I didn't hesitate with my answer. "Loyalty."

"Misplaced loyalty. He doesn't need you. Maybe you're afraid to make your own decisions," he shot back at me.

I never should have tried to engage with him. It was time to counter-attack. "Why did you need my help?"

"When, today?"

"Yes. We've been overworked in the past and you've always done more than keep up."

"Maybe I've gotten tired of doing your work and mine."

"But this *was* your work."

"I've been busy," he said, but he'd become defensive. He was hiding something. Of course, I knew what he'd been doing, or at least *where* he'd been doing it. But I couldn't ask him why he'd been hanging out with drug dealers.

Mary brought our food, but we both ignored it, our eyes locked on each other.

"Too busy to do your work doesn't sound like someone headed for the big leagues." I was enjoying regaining the upper hand. I could almost hear his teeth grinding.

"I could have managed without you. It was Johnson's idea."

"Two months ago you wouldn't have gone along with it. You'd have been at the office until two in the morning if you had to."

"I realized it wasn't appreciated."

We ate our food in silence. I paid the bill and we headed back to the office. I couldn't decide if I'd learned anything or not.

CHAPTER TWENTY-THREE

Shantel called later that afternoon and told me that all the evidence we'd gathered yesterday was tagged, cataloged and on its way to the lab, but it would be weeks before we found out anything. The disadvantage of being a small county is that we rely heavily on other labs for almost all of our work. At least we could tell them whose DNA and fingerprints we were trying to match. That would help.

At five I decided I'd had enough of my day of working with Matt. I spotted Pete coming into the building as I was on my way out.

"I feel like crap," were the first words out of his mouth. He looked like someone whose "Dear John" letter had shown up on the same day that his goldfish died.

"I'm the one who had to spend all day with Matt Greene." I wasn't in a sympathetic mood.

"I just got done re-interviewing all the rape victims," he said heavily.

Okay, his day was worse. "Find out anything?" I asked gently.

"Nope. It ended up just being a matter of checking all the boxes. None of them could pull Conway out of a twenty-picture lineup. A couple of them thought that the objects found in Conway's closet might be related to their cases, but they couldn't be sure. Bottom line is, we're going to have to count on the physical evidence to prove our point."

"Well, it's not like we're going to have to prove Conway's guilt beyond a reasonable doubt. We just have to clear Ayers's name. We can do that by showing that Conway is a probable, even likely, suspect."

"True. Speaking of evidence, did you and Shantel find any smoking guns?"

"We collected a lot of stuff and a fair number of fingerprints, but nothing that jumped out at us. It's just going to take time."

"Because of Nichols's poor performance at the interview, the bosses have decided to keep him off duty until further notice."

"And Dad said that he hired a lawyer. We'll just have to see how it all turns out. I'm heading home," I said.

"I'm going to check-in and deal with some emails, then head for the range. I need to burn some powder." Pete headed for his desk just as my phone went off. It was Dad.

"You need to take Mac for another ride before next weekend," he told me.

Damn it! I'd forgotten about the parade. My mind went into overdrive trying to come up with a way to get out of it. "I'm not sure when I'll have the time," I equivocated.

"How about this weekend?"

"Well... I..." I didn't want to tell him that I was planning on spending at least some of the weekend, as much as I could, with Cara.

"Bring your girlfriend over," he suggested, as if reading my mind. "If she doesn't want to ride Finn, we can borrow one of the neighbor's horses. Jan's got a palomino that's calm as a summer breeze."

"Yeah, okay. I'll ask her," I said reluctantly.

On Thursday afternoon, as Pete and I were typing up reports

and organizing the files on both the rapes and the Ayers shooting, I got a call from Shantel.

"Remember that pool net thingy we collected from the Conway house?" Shantel asked excitedly. She could never have had a career playing poker.

"The one with the handle that was so long we almost couldn't fit it in the car?"

"That's the one. I didn't send it with the rest of the evidence 'cause... Well... I just had a hunch."

"You said the plastic wouldn't hold fingerprints very well."

"That's true. But Marcus and I bagged the whole thing, used superglue and we found a partial."

I sat up at my desk. "No kidding? Does it match Nichols?"

"Good news is, hell yes! But the bad news is it's a couple points short of being a sure thing."

A lawyer would be able to cast doubt on a partial fingerprint that an expert couldn't say with certainty came from the suspect, but we could still use it as leverage. "That'll work for now."

"There's more. I figured it might have been used to push the body underwater, so I went over the netting and came up with some hairs that probably match our body." Her voice was full of glee. I couldn't blame her.

"That's great. Thanks, Shantel," I said sincerely, hanging up the phone.

The new evidence was promising, but still wouldn't hold up very well in court. The deceased used the hot tub regularly and anyone who takes a bath or swims in a pool knows that hairs are constantly coming out and clogging up drains and would probably adhere to a pool skimmer. Still, a prosecutor could use it to paint a picture of how the murder occurred.

Pete and I went into an interview room so we could talk privately about how to proceed.

"It's not enough to charge him. Not yet," Pete said.

"Besides, I think we need to move forward with all three cases. The murder of Conway, for which we have the best evidence. The murder of Ayers, where we have him admitting to the shooting so we just have to prove that he didn't have a justification. And finally the murder of Angie Maitland. That last is going to be the hardest to prove, at least right now."

"And we want to have a strong enough case, and enough charges, that we can plea bargain for the names of any accomplices and still put him away for life."

"Exactly."

"We still have a ways to go."

"Yep. We need to bring the sheriff up to speed and make sure that there's no opportunity for Nichols to flee or to do any more damage."

I was calling Dad before Pete was done talking. He was in Tallahassee at a regional law enforcement meeting and we agreed to get together the next morning. Before I could hang up, he reminded me again about riding Mac.

On Friday we all agreed on how we were going to proceed with Nichols. Of course, Dad and I had high hopes of flipping Nichols to implicate Matt Greene. Shantel arranged to meet with the lab in Tallahassee when they were ready to go over the evidence we had sent them. She wanted to make sure that nothing was overlooked.

My biggest concern was that word would get out. Both the department and the county were small. Everyone had friends and relatives working in the office. Someone might tell Nichols or Matt where the investigation was and where it was headed. But that couldn't be helped. All I could do was worry about it, and I was determined that when I walked out of the office I would leave all my worries behind for the weekend.

Cara pulled some strings at work and was able to swap Saturdays with another vet tech. She was excited about the horseback ride. I drove over early to pick her up.

"Nice," I said, admiring how she looked in jeans and boots. "You look like you know what you're doing."

"I've been on a horse before," she said, raising her eyebrows. "Just try to keep up." She pushed past me with a smile and headed for my car.

Some of her cockiness disappeared on the way to Dad's when I told her he was going to be there.

"Really? Okay, now I'm nervous."

"If it gets too embarrassing and, believe me, with my father it could get very embarrassing, we can redirect his attention to the horses or the barn or Mauser or anything other than our relationship. Besides, you have met him before."

"Yeah, but just at the vet with Mauser and that one time at Christmas. I still don't feel like I *know* him."

"Don't worry about it. Ha, just think what it will be like if your parents ever meet my dad."

She was quiet for a moment while she thought about that and then started laughing so hard I thought I might need to stop the car. "Oh… my… God!" she exclaimed and started laughing again. "I just can't imagine."

Her dad was part-hippy, part-Viking while her mother was all hippy. They lived in a small co-op down near Gainesville. I'd met them both last month when her father had been implicated in a series of murders. Once I'd helped clear his name, I'd gained a friend for life. But picturing my dad alongside her parents *was* pretty comical.

"Are you okay?" I asked as her laughing fit turned into a choking fit.

Finally she caught her breath. "I'm fine. Thank you. I needed that."

As we were getting out of the car, Dad and Mauser came up from the barn. When Mauser saw Cara he lost his mind. He ran straight for her, ears flapping, tongue lolling and his enormous paws thundering across the yard.

"Mauser!" Cara shouted at him as he zoomed past her.

He wheeled around and made several more passes before coming to rest against Cara's side. She rubbed him vigorously, making happy sounds to his panting, wild-eyed face.

"If this was summer he'd have been sitting in the shade or lounging in his wading pool and waited for you to come over to him," Dad said, his chest puffed out with pride. He loved to see people make a fuss over Mauser.

Dad had already gone next door and borrowed the neighbor's palomino, Lucy, so we went straight to the barn. Dad didn't go with us. He just gave me a smile and took Mauser out back to work on some fencing.

We rode Mac and Lucy down the dirt road that ran alongside Dad's property. Finn followed on the inside of the fence as long as he could, giving us a couple whinnies as we rode out of sight. Luckily, Finn and Mac weren't as stable-mated as you would expect. Dad always maintained that since they were twins, each had a special sense about the other and felt comfortable that, even when the other was out of sight, they were both fine.

We didn't talk much. We put the horses through their paces, though neither Mac nor Lucy was very energetic going away from home.

"You're pretty good," I told Cara as Mac and I came up beside her and Lucy.

"Are you really surprised?"

"No." With her love of animals, and knowing that she'd spent part of her early years on a Kentucky horse farm, it wasn't the least bit surprising that she could ride.

"Thank you."

"What for?"

"For trying to understand me."

"I got some good advice from a friend."

"I really want us to give this a chance." She looked over and her eyes grabbed mine.

"I do too," I said.

She smiled and squeezed her legs, pushing Lucy into a

quick-paced trot. With much cajoling, I got Mac to break into a canter, but before we could pass the ladies Cara took Lucy into a full gallop, leaving Mac and me in the dust. We didn't catch up until she had pulled Lucy back down into a walk.

I was about to suggest we turn around when my phone went off.

"Hello?" I asked, just managing to fumble the phone out of its case before the call went to voicemail.

"Is this Deputy Macklin?" asked an officious voice from the other end of the line.

"Yep. What can I do for you?"

"This is Thomas Bryer. I'm acting as Deputy Isaac Nichols's attorney." I had a vague impression of Bryer. He'd represented some of the local law enforcement officers on different cases, mostly civil suits.

"And?"

"Honestly, I'm not happy about this, but he wanted me to call you and ask you to meet him at his house this afternoon."

"I don't understand." I was taken aback. "He wants us to meet at his place? Today?"

"He says he just wants to meet with you. When I pressed him, he insisted. When I asked him why, he said it would be better if he had a chance to discuss things with you first. It makes little sense to me, but he was adamant."

"Pete is the lead investigator. He really needs to be there."

"Just you," Bryer said, not leaving any wiggle room. "Will you meet with him?"

"I guess, yes. What time?" I'd call Pete and discuss it with him, but I couldn't imagine that he wouldn't want me to find out what Nichols had to say.

"Three o'clock."

I looked at my watch. It was one now.

"Where?"

"His house. I'll tell him you'll be there."

"Yes," I said, just before he disconnected. "I have to get back," I told Cara, who nodded.

We tried to enjoy the ride back, but my mind was distracted. I called Pete when we were almost back to Dad's.

"You're calling me from horseback?"

"Yes, and if Mac spooks I'm going to drop my phone so let me tell you why I called."

"Has that horse ever spooked?"

"All horses spook, especially the ones you say never spook. Listen, Nichols wants to meet with me."

"Just you? What's that all about?"

"I don't know. But I told his lawyer that I'd meet Nichols at his house this afternoon."

"Strange. And it was so urgent he had to meet you on a Saturday?"

"Maybe he got word that we've found some evidence. He probably knows we went back out to Conway's house."

"Possibly. Just record the conversation."

"I will if he'll let me. I'll call you as soon as I'm done talking with him."

Cara and I unsaddled the horses, brushed them down and picked their hooves before turning Mac out into the pasture where Finn met him with happy snort.

Dad came out to the barn. "Don't worry about Lucy. I'll walk her back," he told us.

"Where's Mauser?" Cara asked.

"Are you kidding? He was outside for a couple hours this morning, then greeted you. He's holding down the couch. If you listen closely you can hear him snoring." Dad smiled.

"Nichols wants to meet with me," I told him, knowing I was spoiling the mood.

"When?"

I looked at my watch. "In less than an hour. At his house. Alone."

"I don't like that. If he's guilty and knows we're getting close, he might be getting desperate."

"Why pick on me? Pete's been the lead. I think he's more

likely going to propose a deal, and he chose me because he figures I have a direct line to you."

We played out a couple of other thoughts and options, and finally Dad suggested that I have one of the deputies on duty stationed not too far away in case things went south. I agreed.

CHAPTER TWENTY-FOUR

After dropping Cara off, I went by the office and checked in with dispatch, telling them where I was going to be. Mark Edwards was the closest deputy on duty. I called him and gave him a CliffsNotes version of the situation, leaving out the fact that Nichols was suspected in at least two murders. Edwards confirmed that he'd stand-by a couple blocks from Nichols's house until I gave him the all-clear. I thought this was all overkill, but you never know.

I drove up to Nichols's small, ranch-style house. There were toys in the yard, but no sign of kids. Everything seemed quiet. I half expected a disembodied voice to say, *Too quiet*.

As I walked up to the door, the sun went behind the clouds and the temperature felt like it dropped ten degrees. I knocked. Nothing. I looked for a doorbell, but the button I found had been painted over and looked like it hadn't worked in a decade. I tried it anyway. Nothing. I knocked again.

"Isaac, it's Larry. You wanted to meet?" Still no answer.

If I'd been smart I would have called Edwards, but I'm not that smart. Besides, I thought there was a chance that Nichols had gotten cold feet and that I could convince him to talk to me. I thought about walking around the house, but

I decided to try the door first. The knob turned. I opened the door and shouted. Still nothing. Stupidly, I convinced myself that I should just go in a little way and check it out.

I eased my way in, putting my right hand on the butt of my Glock 17.

"Nichols!" Before the echo of his name had faded, I heard sirens. A chill ran up my spine. I moved into the living room and saw Nichols's body lying flopped over on the couch. I didn't need to check his pulse. The back of his head was a bloody mess. In fact, I realized it was still very wet. I pulled my gun and started to clear the house as the sirens stopped outside.

"Hello! Police! Anyone in the house?" a woman shouted from outside. I knew that voice.

"Darl, it's Deputy Macklin," I yelled back, replacing my gun in its holster.

"Macklin! What the hell are you doi—" Her voice stopped midsentence and I knew she'd found Nichols's body. I started back down the hallway to the living room.

"It's me, Darl," I said loudly, my hands half raised. "The house is clear."

She whirled on me, holding her gun at the low ready. "Stay where you are," said Officer Darlene Marks of the Calhoun Police Department. Her whole body vibrated with the adrenaline pulsing through her veins. She was a petite woman in her mid-thirties, and the gun in her hand looked very large. I raised my hands higher.

"I need backup. I'm at 456 Gator Creek Drive. The owner of the house appears to be deceased and there is an off-duty deputy on the scene," she said into the radio strapped to her shoulder as she held the gun in her strong hand a little higher. To me she said, "Larry, don't move and keep your hands where I can see them."

She moved back so that she could watch me and the front door at the same time. Dispatch told her that other officers were on the way.

I looked at Darl, trying to remain calm. She'd explained

to me once that she had to call herself Darl because Darlene sounded too much like "darling" and just didn't sound tough enough for police work.

"Look, I'm here because I received a call from Nichols's attorney that Nichols wanted to meet with me. I arrived just a few minutes before you did." I shouldn't have been talking, but it's hard not to try and explain yourself when you're caught in a compromising position.

Luckily, Deputy Edwards had heard the sirens and figured things out. He was the next one through the door.

"Deputy Edwards! I'm coming in," he announced from the front door.

"Stay outside," Darl ordered.

"We could all move outside," I suggested.

"I don't know if the house is clear yet," she said reasonably. From the living room she had a view of the back hallway, the murder scene and the kitchen. In this situation, I would have told any officer to not assume that the officer I found on scene was innocent and to remain in a position to protect the crime scene until a supervisor arrived. She couldn't take my gun without risking contaminating evidence. It was a tricky scenario and I couldn't really fault her for how she handled it.

After what seemed like an eternity, her lieutenant arrived. He bagged my gun and took me outside.

Calhoun's police department is so small that I wasn't surprised by who arrived on the scene next. Chief Charles Maxwell pulled up to the house in a black Cadillac Escalade, blue lights flashing on the dash.

"What the hell is going on?" he asked me. I was surprised there wasn't more gloating in his tone.

I explained about the phone call and what I had found when I arrived.

"If I call Bryer, he'll back up your story?" Maxwell asked snidely. I had to bite back the urge to tell him that it wasn't a story.

"Yes."

"You realize this puts me between a rock and a hard place?" he asked.

"Honestly, I was thinking more about Nichols, who's dead. I'm thinking that he's probably the one coming out of this the worst."

"Did you shoot him?" he asked while trying to stare me down.

"No, I didn't shoot him. He was dead when I got here."

"You were found here with the dead body. I understand that you've been investigating the shooting that took place last week. The one that Nichols was involved in."

Maxwell had a habit of asking poorly worded questions or sometimes, like this one, making statements that posed as questions. I had to restrain myself from coming back with snappy answers that would just piss him off.

"I had reason to be here. I assume that he wanted to talk with me about that investigation."

"Do you usually meet with a suspect in his home at his bidding on a Saturday?"

"No. I'm not going to go into details about an ongoing investigation. You know that I can't, and that I probably should remain silent. But I'm trying to be cooperative."

"And you know that I should be treating you like a suspect, but I'm trying to be civil." He came in closer so that he could whisper. "Everyone knows that I'm running for sheriff against your father. If I do anything that could be construed as… less than tactful with you, it could be seen as a political move against your family. I'm not going to give your father the opportunity to play that against me."

He turned his head and watched the officers milling about in the front yard. "And, honestly, I don't think you did it. We received an anonymous call about a shooting. Dispatch sent Officer Marks to investigate."

"The only time we get an anonymous phone call when a crime is taking place is when someone is trying to frame someone else for it."

"Exactly, and they called us instead of the sheriff's office because they wanted us to respond, knowing that I'm in a political fight with your father. Oh, and did I mention that the call didn't come in through the 911 system?"

"If it had, then a deputy might have been dispatched," I said thoughtfully.

"Yep. They wanted police, not the sheriff's office."

The man was annoyingly egotistical, but he wasn't stupid.

"Still leaves me with a dilemma. What do I do with you?"

As if on cue, I saw my father's truck pull up behind Maxwell's Caddy. Dad jumped out and strode over to us. Maxwell stopped talking to me and turned to face a very angry Ted Macklin.

"What the hell—" Dad started and Maxwell raised both his hands as though he knew that one hand wouldn't be enough to stop my father.

"You can stop right there and keep your temper under control."

I don't know if Maxwell knew it or not, but telling Dad to keep his temper in check was one of the best ways to send him over the edge. But Dad stopped where he was and I could see his inner struggle to control his anger.

"Two things," Dad said, his eyes blazing in the afternoon light. "One, that is one of my deputies who's dead in there," he said, pointing toward the house. "And that means something to me. Second, my son was not involved in this shooting."

"First, Nichols was a law enforcement officer and I've met and worked with him before. I take his death as seriously as you do. I will do whatever is necessary to discover what happened to him this afternoon. Second, while I am reasonably sure that your son did not pull the trigger that killed Nichols, I'm going to treat him like a suspect until we have the evidence to clear him."

As Maxwell spoke these last words I could see the color rise in Dad's face. *When he explodes, will they be able to pick it up on seismographs?* I wondered.

"Think, Macklin, if we do this right and there is evidence

that backs up your son's story, then he won't have a shadow hanging over him. But on the other hand, if I just turn him loose to your custody, there are some folks who will always wonder if there was something fishy going on. Now, I'm going to bag his hands until I can do a gunpowder residue test. And we'll take him to FDLE to have the tests performed. Fair enough?"

I could see Dad processing this. Reluctantly he said, "Makes sense."

"His gun has already been bagged and will be tested, though I think we found the murder weapon under the coffee table. I would hope that after the powder residue test, Larry will give a statement. If everything checks out, I'll release him tonight."

"That's reasonable," Dad said grudgingly. "What about the investigation? It was my deputy who died."

"If I'm comfortable that Larry wasn't involved in the shooting, then we'll discuss how to move forward with the investigation. At this moment in time, the case is mine." This sounded like Maxwell's final answer, but Dad wasn't quite ready to drop it.

"I want—" he started.

"Nothing right now. Don't push me or I'll see that this whole thing gets turned over to FDLE."

This stopped Dad. If the Florida Department of Law Enforcement was called in, they'd want the files on everything—the rapes, the shooting—and they'd push until they'd ferreted out our suspicions about Matt. Dad wasn't about to have all that taken out of his hands.

"Fine. For now." There was a huge bark from behind him. I looked over and saw Mauser hanging his jowly face out the window of Dad's truck.

"I see you brought backup," I said to Dad.

"Damn straight."

Maxwell looked like he couldn't decide if we were joking or not. I'd heard that he wasn't a dog person.

He turned and called for one of his officers to bring over

161

some large evidence bags and tape. After sealing my hands, Maxwell took me over to his car. Dad stood there watching helplessly as I was treated like a suspect. As reasonable as Maxwell was being, I could tell that the reptile part of Dad's brain was going to want payback someday.

CHAPTER TWENTY-FIVE

I woke up Sunday morning to a call from Dad.

"After I texted you I came straight home. I was in bed by one o'clock," I told him.

"I came into the office this morning." He let that hang in the air for a minute. "I checked the tracker data on Matt. He was a block over from Nichols's house during the murder."

"I can't decide whether I'm surprised or not."

"I think this is close to a smoking gun," Dad stated flatly. "He was off duty. Of course, there's a chance he has a good reason for being there, but the coincidences are stacking up."

"What we need is some physical evidence."

"I talked with Maxwell after he turned you loose last night. He's being reasonable. Agreed to sharing information on Nichols's case. Of course, he knows that he doesn't have the manpower or resources to handle this on his own."

That was very true. The Calhoun Police Department amounted to about a dozen officers. The sheriff's office provided most of the backup for them, and we did almost all of the violent crime investigations.

"You aren't going to give him any of the background information?" I asked, already knowing the answer.

"No. I'll tell him that we have reason to believe there was

a dispute between Nichols and one of our officers. Then we'll provide him with Matt's DNA and fingerprints and see if there's a match with any of the forensics they pulled out of Nichols's house."

Cara called later and I explained how I'd spent my Saturday night. She offered to come over and bring some food for lunch. "That sounds awesome," I told her.

We had a late brunch of whole grain chocolate chip pancakes with maple syrup that her dad got from a farm in Vermont.

"It was bad?" she asked as we washed dishes.

I knew this was one of the small tests. The relationship equivalent of a pop quiz. Had I learned anything from our troubles last week?

"Yeah, pretty bad. I wouldn't say that Nichols was a friend, but I knew him pretty well. Seeing him like that was… disturbing."

"I'm sorry." She put her hand on my arm. "Did they actually arrest you?"

"No. They just had to eliminate me as a suspect. Maxwell was pretty decent about it in his own pompous, in-your-face way."

"Do you think Nichols killed himself?" she asked, taking us onto shakier ground.

"I really can't talk about an ongoing investigation."

"I understand." And she sounded like she meant it.

We finished the dishes in peaceful silence.

"Let's clean up the yard," I said as we left the kitchen.

"Is that supposed to be a fun activity?"

"I need to work off those pancakes and there's a lot of deadfall out there from last year. We had a little rain the other day, so things aren't too dry and we can burn it."

"I guess, if you think that sounds like a good time."

We soon had a couple piles of leaves and branches burning in the crisp winter's air. It felt good to be near the fire, and better to be near Cara.

Finished with as much work as we were going to do, we sat in two old lawn chairs under the live oaks and watched the fires burn down.

"There's just something about the smell of wood smoke on a winter's day," she said

"Puts you in a romantic mood?"

"No, it makes me think of marshmallows." She smiled a wicked grin. "And s'mores!"

"From your time in the Girl Scouts?"

"Ha, are you kidding? My folks considered the Girl Scouts a proto-Fascist movement. And they never would have let me have all those processed sugars and dyes. But I had a friend whose parents were more permissive, and when I'd stay over at her house in the winter her parents would build a fire in the backyard. Ann and I would camp out in a tent and cook a wonderful dinner of sugar, chocolate and graham crackers. I felt like I was a kid in Willy Wonka's factory."

"You go get the goods and I'll stir up the fire," I told her.

Cara hopped up, gave me a quick peck on the cheek and headed for her car. There was a small store a couple miles up the road. I found some good sticks for marshmallow roasting and, when she got back, we made a mess and laughed ourselves into convulsions as the marshmallows went up in flames.

Once our blood sugar was up to dangerous levels, we leaned back in our chairs and gazed at the sparks from the fire as they sailed up to mingle with the stars.

"You realize that we can't live on chocolate chip pancakes and s'mores?" I told Cara, reaching out to take her hand. Our fingers were sticky from the marshmallows and chocolate.

"Don't be a spoilsport," she admonished me. "I know that I'll have to wake up from this dream eventually, but not yet."

I didn't tell her that my father had called while she was

gone. He just wanted to know how I was doing and to make sure I would come straight to his office in the morning. I assured him that was my plan. We had to deal with Matt Greene, and whatever we decided to do was going to be fraught with pitfalls. I managed to push those worries aside long enough to enjoy the rest of my evening with Cara.

I woke up feeling better than I should have. I'd gotten a good night's rest after Cara left, but I had a bunch of crap to deal with as soon as I got to the office. The more I woke up and thought about it, the worse I felt. There were a million questions that I'd been willing to ignore yesterday, but I wasn't going to have that luxury today. It was not going to be a fun day.

Sure enough, as I pulled into the parking lot I could see two reporters waiting at the front door to ambush whoever came up. When they recognized me they quivered with excitement.

"Deputy Macklin!" they shouted in unison. I thought about brushing past them, but decided that I could manage a more diplomatic response.

"Yes." I held up my hand. "I know that you all have questions, and you know that I'm not in a position to answer them."

"Just a couple of questions," a reporter from one of the Tallahassee TV affiliates said as though I hadn't spoken. "We understand that you were first on the scene of Deputy Nichols's death. Was it a suicide?"

"His death is currently under investigation." I turned and started up the few steps to the front door, listening to the two reporters shouting questions at my back.

"I told them to hang outside," the desk sergeant mumbled as I walked by. He wore a black band over his star. I realized I needed to find a black ribbon to tie around my upper arm. Nothing had been proven against Nichols and, as much I was sure that he was crooked, I needed to act otherwise.

I went straight to the sheriff's office. Dad's assistant barely looked up. She was wearing black. I knocked once and went in. Dad was sitting behind his enormous desk, looking over a pile of reports.

"Maxwell sent over the reports he's gotten from his men. I had our deputies who showed up at the scene send over their reports to him."

"Has Maxwell received the autopsy report on Nichols?"

"It was in the stuff he sent over. Nothing definitive. The gun was placed in the mouth and that's consistent with a suicide. However, there was some bruising around his lips that suggests someone might have forced the gun into his mouth. Some alcohol in his system, but he wasn't drunk. Of course, it will be a little while before a full toxicology report is ready. So pretty much, blah, blah and blah," Dad finished, looking exasperated.

"So?"

"So, this is really a damn mess."

"We know that Matt was involved," I stated.

"*Suspect* it."

"We have to question him. Find out if he had a reason to be there. Remember, that's not the only coincidence," I argued.

"I'm well aware of that. But we have to be careful. All we have now is a dead deputy who was somehow involved with a serial rapist. But we don't know what the exact connection is between Nichols and Conway. Nichols, at the very least, shot Ayers in cold blood and is complicit in the murder of Angie Maitland, but we don't have much physical evidence to back that up. We do have some solid evidence that he was at Conway's house, though it's not good enough for court and we've lost the opportunity to confront him about that."

"The case doesn't sound great when you put it like that. Or, I should say, the individual parts don't look good. Together, though, that's another matter. From the right perspective it becomes pretty obvious that Nichols was involved up to his teeth."

"Pretty obvious is not a legal phrase. Arresting him because we thought he was pretty obviously guilty would not fly. The hell of it is, we can't arrest him because he's dead. He will never be guilty of anything. He'll receive a funeral with honors and his family will get his death benefits. The icing on the cake is that I'll have to stand up at his funeral and say nice things about him, suspecting that he was the scum of the earth." Dad finished this rant and slumped back in his chair. He wasn't taking it well.

I sat down in a chair across from his desk and leaned in. "What's important is that we still have a killer on the loose. A dirty cop. Stopping him has to be our top priority."

Dad looked at me with hard, flinty eyes. The look I remembered from childhood that meant I was pushing him too hard.

"I don't need you to tell me what our priorities are. I hired both of these men. One of them has escaped justice. I won't allow the other one to do the same. I'll remind you that if we make a move too soon, we might just end up watching him walk."

"I'm not trying to tell you what to do. I wish I wasn't involved in this at all. But I'm the one that discovered Matt sneaking around with the Thompsons. I feel responsible too."

Dad's eyes softened a bit. "And I appreciate the fact that you have a sense of duty. I'm proud of you. But the decision rests on my shoulders."

"What about bringing in some more people? Pete?"

"Not Pete. Everyone in the department knows about the bad blood between Pete and Matt. A defense attorney would be able to paint anything that Pete did as a form of payback."

"So who can we bring into the investigation?"

"Who could we trust?"

"Matt doesn't have a lot of friends. Heck, he really doesn't have any close friends in the department."

"People are funny, though. Particularly in law enforcement. Some of that thin blue line stuff is nonsense, but not all of it. No, the only option is to bring in FDLE. Of course, at this point I could be criticized for not bringing in outside investigators sooner."

"So…"

"Once we open that can of worms, we better be prepared to fish. That's all I'm saying." He leaned back and closed his eyes.

We sat like that for several minutes before he spoke again. "There's no way around it. I'll call FDLE and ask them to come in and oversee the investigation of Matt."

CHAPTER TWENTY-SIX

I spent the rest of Monday organizing my notes in preparation for a meeting with FDLE. It was frustrating not being able to tell Pete what we were doing and I felt as if I was betraying our friendship. But no one else could know until FDLE decided how we should proceed. I felt especially bad for Dad. Not only did he have to admit that the department needed outside help, but it would require that he turn over control of the investigation into Matt's behavior. Dad was a control freak. This had to be gut-wrenching for him.

He called me at four. "They want to meet tomorrow. I've arranged for them to come out to my house around noon. I want you to be there, and bring a thumb drive with copies of all the files they'll need. I'll have the tracking information on Matt." Dad's voice was flat and he hung up as soon as I acknowledged his requests.

Tuesday was cloudy and rainy, signaling a cold front. I got to Dad's at eleven-thirty and helped him organize and make copies of the paper files. To distract himself he talked about the Great Americans parade coming up on Saturday. Every time I tried to bring up Matt Greene, he changed the subject back to whether he needed to body clip Finn, or how he needed to clean all of his leather parade gear.

At five minutes before noon a professional knock on the front door was met by ear-shattering barks from Mauser, who ran to the door, jumping up and down on his front paws in excitement. Dad tried to body-block Mauser as he opened the door, but the huge beast was determined to give the visitors a full Great Dane greeting.

The two agents standing on the porch looked like they'd been sent by central casting for MIB auditions. The first agent squeezed past Dad and Mauser and suffered through the greeting ritual. The second agent, who looked strong enough to bench-press two Mausers, ran ten feet back from the door, shaking his head vigorously.

"Hell no," he said, trying to regain his composure. "Sir, could you put your dog in another room, please?" he asked, shaking his head.

Dad gave him a cold look, but finally nodded. "Come on, boy-o," he said to Mauser, who had to be leashed and lured with a peanut butter Kong before Dad could get him into the bedroom. Even then, we could hear pitiful whining as the big lunk bemoaned his cruel imprisonment.

The meeting didn't take long. We presented our evidence, weak as it was, and they listened. They took all the files that we gave them, said they'd review them and get back with us. That was it.

"Did they really just tell us to do nothing?" I asked incredulously as Dad let Mauser out of the bedroom. The big moose tried to crawl into my lap and looked at Dad reproachfully, still holding a grudge for being locked up.

"That's sure the hell what it sounded like. I better hear from them soon."

"Is that odd?"

"I've never called them in to investigate an internal matter. Usually, if you hear about them getting into a department's business, it's with a very heavy hand. But they've probably been involved for a while before it goes public." I could tell that he was no more satisfied by the agents' reactions than I was.

"We'll give them a couple of days. If they haven't gotten back to me by then…" He let the sentence trail off ominously.

On Wednesday I went about business as usual, trying to avoid Matt at all costs. Pete and I worked on a routine caseload of burglaries, robberies and assaults. Once I started digging, most of them were less exciting than the charges made them sound.

Dad called late in the afternoon. "I just heard from Maxwell. FDLE asked to be copied on all their reports pertaining to Nichols's death."

"So they're doing something."

"Exactly. They're doing something. But mostly what they're doing is leaving us hanging with a dangerous officer on duty," he said. I could tell he was frustrated at having given up control of the situation. "If I don't hear from them this afternoon, I'll call them in the morning. I've got Johnson giving Matt the lowest priority cases."

Pete and I were at lunch at Winston's on Thursday when Dad called again.

"They told me to sit on it through the weekend. They're reviewing all aspects of the case and will update me then, blah, blah, blah. Maybe I'm getting too old for this job. I should have brought Matt in myself and let the chips fall where they may. Whatever happened, at least he wouldn't be a deputy in our county anymore." This was the most depressed I'd heard Dad sound since my mother died.

"You know that wouldn't have been the right thing to do. You took the harder path, but it's also the right path," I said, trying to believe my own words. Pete looked up curiously from his cheeseburger. I shook my head, trying to indicate that this was nothing serious.

"I hear you. Monday. I'll give them until Monday, but I'm not letting Matt carry around our star any longer than that." We'd reached bedrock. After Monday, there'd be no talking Dad out of taking action.

"What time do I need to be at your place on Saturday?" I just wanted to change the subject.

"We have to be lined up for the parade by nine-thirty. I told Bob to have everyone there at nine. If you get to my place by seven-thirty, that'll give us enough time to brush the horses down and get them in the trailer. Have you cleaned all your gear?" He was quick to slip into parent mode. I didn't mind it today.

"Yes, father. I have my gear all cleaned and laid out."

"Be on time," he said and disconnected.

"Parade?" Pete asked.

"Yeah."

"I'm working the line," Pete said, looking grim. He never liked squeezing into his uniform. But for one of the largest parades of the year, every deputy on duty would be working the streets. I realized Matt would also to be working in uniform that morning. The thought made me lose my appetite and I pushed my half-eaten chicken breast sandwich to the edge of the table.

I spent Thursday evening watching a movie at Cara's. I don't remember what it was. My mind kept dwelling on Matt, Nichols, Ayers, Conway and the rapes. And, yes, I told her that's why I seemed preoccupied, and she was good with that. At least I was doing better with the relationship stuff.

Isaac Nichols's funeral was on Friday. Dad wore his uniform, but not his dress uniform. Otherwise, he did his duty and managed to give a decent eulogy. The flag was presented to Nichols's wife and children. Everyone was grim-faced, though some of us for reasons other than grief.

CHAPTER TWENTY-SEVEN

I was out the door Saturday morning by seven, thinking: *It is way too damn cold for this.* When I got to his house, Dad already had the horses in the crossties.

"You're lucky. I washed them yesterday afternoon. All we need to do is brush 'em and wipe them down," Dad told me as he headed for the tack room. "I hooked the trailer up last night and put everything in it." I was pretty sure he was telling me all this so that I'd feel properly guilty for not thinking that I needed to come over last night and help him get ready. He really knew how to dish it out.

Mac looked as excited to be awake as I was. Dad tossed me a brush and I started grooming. Just as we were finishing, a car pulled into the driveway.

"Who's that?"

"Jamie. I told you, he's going to walk Mauser with the Sheriff's Explorers," Dad said.

I didn't contradict him, but he'd never mentioned that Jamie and Mauser were going to be in the parade too. I would have warned the Explorers that they didn't want to share the stage with Mauser. The big ham would get all the attention.

When I saw the lanky blond-haired kid, I remembered

him from the Explorers. I thought if he let his hair grow out, he'd look just like Shaggy. Throw a little brown paint on Mauser and they'd be ready to ride in the Mystery Machine.

He greeted me with a wave and turned his attention to Dad. "I'm going to take Mauser for a short walk and then head out with him, if that's okay."

"Sure, he's been out for his morning constitutional already and had breakfast. I had to drag his ass out of bed."

Jamie nodded, turned and half jogged toward the house.

"Nice kid. Parents are a damn mess," Dad said and untied Finn, who was his usual snorty self, always on alert. "We'll load Finn on first and Mac will follow."

I hated it when Dad acted like I'd never done something I'd done a dozen times before. Keeping my thoughts to myself, I untied Mac and loaded him up. Once the horses were in the trailer, we put on our dress uniforms and headed for town.

When we pulled up to the staging area in the shopping center parking lot, Bob Muller was already there with some of the posse. He told Dad that he expected about a dozen riders.

We took the horses out of the trailer and tied them up to the side.

"What are you looking at?" Dad asked. I realized I'd been staring at a spot in the parking lot.

"That's where Ayers's car was parked."

"I remember."

"I know now why it wasn't parked," I said, as much to myself as to Dad.

"Huh? What do you mean?"

"That night I noticed that it wasn't pulled into a parking space, even though the lines are very clear."

"There wasn't anyone else here. It was nighttime and the parking lot was empty."

"Yes, but people usually park in the spaces even if there

aren't any other cars around. It's a habit."

"But he didn't."

"That's right. You know the one time you don't bother about how you park in a parking lot?" I didn't wait for him to answer. "When a deputy pulls you over. A driver just wants to stop the car and find out what he's being stopped for."

"You think Nichols pulled Ayers over."

"Exactly. Nichols pulled him over and got him to get into his patrol car with some excuse, or by drawing his gun on him, and then he drove him around to the back of store."

"Shame we'll never get to prosecute Nichols," he said sadly.

As I walked back to the truck to get my gun belt, my phone rang. I looked at the phone; it was Eddie. I thought about letting it go to voicemail, but couldn't bring myself to do it.

"What?" I asked brusquely.

"Bad, really bad. Right now." He wasn't making sense.

"Eddie, I don't have time for this. I'll call—"

"No! You have to listen to me!" he shouted.

"Okay, make it quick."

"The parade. Something bad is going down. I don't know everything, but it's that bad cop."

"What do you mean, it's the bad cop?" I was trying to shout and whisper at the same time. I really didn't want to screw with Dad's head this morning, especially since Eddie hadn't contacted me in almost two weeks. Plus, he might just have been high. But what if he did know something?

"I heard them talking. Someone is going down at the parade."

"You had better not be screwing around."

"I'm clean, I'm sober. It might be your dad. Seriously. I'm scared." He sounded scared. He also sounded sober.

"How do you know that it involves their deputy?"

"They said it. They said their guy had taken out their other guy and was going to get a big payoff for finishing the job this morning."

I started to ask how and where he'd heard this, but decided that it didn't matter. He'd never flat-out lied to me.

"Okay. I'll take care of it."

"I told you I'd come through."

"We'll see, Eddie. Don't do anything stupid and I'll get back to you."

I hung up and looked over at Dad, who was talking to Bob. *What should I tell him?* I wondered. *Nothing. It's my informant and my problem to deal with.* If I did it on my own, Dad could disavow all knowledge and toss me to the media wolves.

"Dad, I've got to run back to the office," I told him as he put his saddle on Finn.

"You want me to unhook the trailer?"

"No, I'll just borrow one of the other officers' cars." He gave me an odd look and opened his mouth to ask a question.

"Cara needs me to run an errand," I said and he shut his mouth. Men are always willing to believe that women will make unreasonable demands.

"Well, hurry back," he said grumpily.

I stepped into the back of the horse trailer for a minute where no one could see me and removed the small handgun, a subcompact 1911, from my ankle holster. I made sure the safety was on and slipped it into my pocket where it would be more accessible.

When I'd looked at a list of parade assignments, I'd made a point to see where Matt was going to be stationed along the parade route. At the time I thought I was just obsessing on him. Now I was glad I'd made a note of it. He was at a barricade on a cross street about two blocks from the shopping center.

I walked as fast as I could while trying *not* to look like I was in a hurry. A block away, I saw Matt standing near Deputy Edwards. I greeted both of them as I walked up. Edwards smiled broadly and said, "Howdy." I got a subtle glower from Matt.

"Matt, is that your car?" I asked, pointing to the Toyota that I knew was his.

"Yeah."

"The sheriff needs me to get his belt from the station. He was cleaning it yesterday and left it there. Would you drive me so I can go pick it up?"

Matt looked from me to Edwards. I could tell that he wanted to tell Edwards to do it, but couldn't quite work out a good enough excuse.

"Let's hurry," he said, turning toward his car.

We didn't talk on the way to the station.

"Go ahead and park it," I told him when he pulled into the lot.

"How long are you going to be?"

"Dad wanted me to get some other things. I'll need your help," I told him, trying to give it just the right tone. Friendly, but not too friendly.

He parked, got out and was halfway to the front door before I caught up with him. Neither of us said anything to Sergeant Dill Kirby, who was working the front desk.

"He left the stuff in here," I told Matt as I opened the interrogation room door. Apparently he smelled a rat and stopped short of the door.

"What—" He stopped when he saw the gun in my hand.

"Matt Greene, I'm holding you for questioning regarding the murder of Isaac Nichols."

"What the hell are you talking about?"

I reached out and took his gun out of his holster while holding mine close and tight into him. If he'd moved, I would have shot him. "Get in the room."

We stared at each other for a couple of moments. He looked around, but the office was deserted. With few other options, he went in the room.

Once in the room I handcuffed his arm to the desk and searched him for additional weapons.

"Let me make a phone call," Matt said through clenched

teeth.

"Not right now." Who would he call? The Thompsons?

"You can't arrest me. You have no evidence."

"I'm holding you as a material witness. I'll see about charges when I get back from the parade."

I took all of his belongings and put them in an evidence bag and sealed it.

"Give me my phone, damn it!" he yelled, dramatically rattling his shackles.

"You'll get you phone call when I get back from the parade," I said, leaving the room.

I found the desk sergeant standing in the hall where he could watch the door to the interrogation room and the front door. I greeted him.

"What's going on, Larry?" Kirby asked. He was the longest serving member of the Adams County Sheriff's Office. Forty years and counting. Semi-retired now, he came in and worked the desk on his good days, particularly when we were strapped for manpower. His back was a bit bent and his balance not as good as it used to be, but his grip was still like a steel vice. He still had the power of the stare too. I'd seen punks wet themselves under pressure from his stare.

"I'm holding Matt Greene."

"Holding him? For what? How long?" Kirby asked, not without a gleam in those powerful eyes.

"For the next couple of hours. With a little luck, I'll be arresting him later. Right now, I'm going to move him to one of the holding cells. I don't want you to let him near a phone. I'll be back here as soon as the parade is over."

This was a little tricky because Kirby technically outranked me, so he could overrule me if he thought I was making a mistake. But, as a rule, patrol followed the instructions of an investigator.

"If this goes south I don't want you to get in trouble, so I'm putting this in writing." And I did just that, making it a point that I was instructing Kirby that he could damage my investigation if he allowed Greene to have access to anyone from the outside until I returned.

"My pleasure. I never did like the stuck-up prick," Kirby said.

I handed him the evidence bag with Matt's belongings, then placed Matt in a holding cell.

"You're an idiot. You and your father are going to regret this. Give me my damn phone and I'll settle this right now."

I made sure the door of his cell was locked and left him kicking the bars and cursing me.

CHAPTER TWENTY-EIGHT

I made it back to the staging area as Dad finished saddling Mac.

"Where the hell have you been?" he asked, not giving me a chance to answer before he went to mount the excited Finn.

I had only a few qualms about not telling him what I'd done. I put on Mac's bridle, telling myself I was protecting Dad from any fallout from the premature arrest.

Once mounted, I had a chance to look around. I saw Mauser and Jamie with the rest of the Sheriff's Explorers. They were surrounded by the usual Mauser fan club. Jamie had his hands full controlling the monster dog while answering a million questions about how much Mauser weighed, what he ate and where he slept.

Dad rode up alongside me. "We'll be up front with the departmental flags. Let's ride with the flagbearers for a bit, get the horses used to the flapping noise."

I tried to look over the crowd as we moved to the front of the posse. If you have to scout a crowd, there's no better place to do it than from the back of a horse. Everything looked normal. Unfortunately, with the cool weather, everyone was wearing a coat, which made it impossible to tell if they were concealing a weapon. I realized that taking Matt out of the equation hadn't eliminated all the threats. The Thompsons could get someone else if they noticed that Matt wasn't here. I had to warn Dad. Or at least give him a heads-up.

"I got a warning from my CI that someone might try something during the parade."

"Was it that vague?"

"Yes. There was a little more to it, but I took care of it."

He shrugged, too distracted by the parade formation to press for details. "There's always a risk of someone doing something stupid when you get a crowd of people together. Your CI was probably just stringing you along. I wouldn't worry about, but thanks for the warning."

Once the parade was lined up, I was pleased to see that we weren't behind or in front of the fire engines. Two years ago I thought I'd permanently lost half my hearing from them blaring their horns every two minutes as the parade moved along. This year we had the high school band in front of us and the Sheriff's Explorers behind. If I looked back past our riders, I could see Mauser weaving from right to left, making sure that everyone got a good look at him.

I heard the Grand Marshal's starter gun go off and the front of the parade began to move. The wind was blowing enough to make all the flags flutter in high style as each group stepped off in turn.

The route was intelligently designed as a giant circle so that we'd end up where we started. There'd been a couple years where we would finish a mile-long parade only to have to walk back a mile to our cars and trailers.

Along the route we were shouted at by friends, and Dad received some encouragement in his reelection, as well as some catcalls from people who still thought he'd let a rapist loose. I waved to a grumpy-looking Pete, who was trying to keep a large group of kids from running into the street. A block later, I heard a shout and turned to see Cara waving at us.

We'd finished most of the route and were coming to the intersection where I'd picked up Matt. I looked ahead but couldn't see Deputy Edwards. He was probably wondering where Matt had disappeared to. *How am I going to handle Matt? How am I going to break the news to Dad?* I couldn't think of any good options.

Mac's head jerked up, alerting me to the oddest thing. A tall woman was stumbling out of the crowd, shouting something I couldn't quite make out.

"Wrong... Look... Run!" was all I could make out. She started waving her purse and coat in the air, causing Mac to shy away from her. We bumped into the other horses, who were equally spooked. Then a rifle shot cracked the air. The sheriff's department flag fell down on Mac's head, causing him to throw his neck around and dance erratically. I struggled to control him while looking for the shooter.

Everyone had started yelling and running once they realized that someone was shooting. There was a second shot and I heard someone shout behind me, but I'd seen the muzzle flash and cued Mac into a canter. The shot had come from some bushes near the intersection where Matt had been posted. As Mac and I got closer, Deputy Edwards came running toward us with a rifle up to his shoulder.

"I think it came from over there!" he shouted, waving behind him. But he didn't fool me. I'd seen him step out from the very spot I'd seen the muzzle flash.

When he realized I was onto him, he pointed the rifle toward me. His next shot went so close to my head that I heard it go by, causing me to flinch and jerk the reins. Mac stumbled and I rolled over his shoulder and onto the ground.

Back on my feet, I could see Edwards standing in front of a man lying on the street. I started toward them and saw the most amazing tableau I could have imagined. Dad lay in the street, holding his silver 1911 pointed at Edwards, whose rifle was trained on my father. Standing almost on top of Dad was Mauser, with a grim face and curled lip. His eyes

183

were locked on Edwards, his tail stiff and pointing straight up and a growl coming from deep in his throat. The posse surrounded Dad, each of them holding a gun pointed at Edwards. That's when I realized that I was also holding my gun.

A small crowd was still left, all of them watching the scene play out with their mouths hanging open. For a few moments there was nothing but silence, then my dad's voice sounded loud and strong.

"Edwards, you better just put that rifle on the ground, slowly, otherwise the fellas at Marshall's Funeral Home are going to have a hell of a job making your corpse presentable."

Edwards took his eye off of Dad and seemed to notice everyone else for the first time. Tunnel vision—it's a thing. He made his decision and gently lowered the rifle to the ground. I walked up to him, pulled his hands behind him and cuffed him. Another deputy took him away.

That's when I looked over at Dad and noticed that there was blood on his side.

"You've been shot," I said, kneeling down beside him. Mauser tried to lick my face and, when I pushed him away, he laid down next to Dad.

"I'm fine. It just grazed me. It's my ass that hurts. Go get the horses."

I found Mac and Finn across the street, both trying to find something edible on a frost-bitten lawn. I took them back to the trailer and left them munching contentedly from a hay bag as if nothing had happened.

Pete was waiting for me when I got back to Dad. There were paramedics swarming all around him since many of them had been in the parade. They cut Dad's shirt away and tended to his wound while he gave orders to anyone close enough to hear him.

"He's going to be fine," Pete told me, dragging me away. "What the hell is going on? Dill told me that you're holding Matt."

My heart was hammering in my chest. What had I done?

"Let me go check on Dad and fill him in," I told Pete.

Dad was trying to get up on his feet, much to the annoyance of the EMT's.

"I'm fine," he said, trying to push them away. "Barely even broke the skin. I shouldn't have fallen off my horse."

Most of them knew him and realized there was no point in arguing with him. Jamie had the other end of Mauser's leash again and was trying to get the dog to give Dad room enough to stand.

"I need to talk to you," I said and he nodded.

"I want to go see Finn and Mac." He started hobbling toward the trailer. "My damn butt hurts worse than the bullet wound," he mumbled.

"I've done something stupid."

He looked up at me. "Well, you were right about something happening at the parade."

"I was wrong about who. I got a call from Eddie, my CI, saying that our mole was going to do something today. I thought it was Matt. So I put him in a holding cell before the parade."

"You did what?!"

"I—"

"I heard you. You arrested Matt without telling me! Who else knew about this?" He raised his voice loud enough that a few of the folks standing around were looking over at us.

"No one. I did it on my own."

"Are you crazy? What the hell did you think you were doing?" He held up his hand. "Don't answer that."

"I'm going to talk to him now."

"No, you aren't," he stated flatly. "Pete!" he yelled.

Pete hustled his bulk over to us. "Sir!" Pete knew when to be respectful.

"You're in charge of this investigation. He," he pointed at me, "is not to be involved."

"What I did—" I started to explain.

"No, don't go there. What you did was withhold

information from me. By doing that, you took the responsibility for all of this." He waved his hand around. "But I'm the one who's ultimately responsible. I am. You don't have the judgment to make calls like this. Damn it, people could have died."

Every word he said was true. The only thing I could do was grovel. "Please, just let me sit in on the interviews. I won't participate in any way. But I need to see how badly I screwed up."

Dad looked at me, his breathing heavy and his face pained. Whether it was from the shooting, the fall or from the mess I had created for him, I couldn't tell.

"Okay," was all he said, waving his hand dismissively.

I turned to Pete. "I'll unsaddle the horses, get them loaded and meet you at the office."

"Go on. Bob will help me with the horses," Dad said, not looking at me.

CHAPTER TWENTY-NINE

I tried to explain everything to Pete as we drove to the office. He made sympathetic sounds, but he looked hurt when I told him about our suspicions about Matt… and how long we'd had them.

Dill Kirby looked up when we came in. "What the hell happened?"

"We'll fill you in later," Pete told him as we went through the inner doors.

We found Matt pacing up and down in the holding cell.

"Look who's here. The dynamic duo. Did you bring my property?"

"I'll go get it," I said sheepishly.

I met Pete and Matt as they were walking back to the interview room. "Let's talk in here," Pete said, opening the door.

Once seated, Matt held up his cell phone. "Before we go any further, I need to make a call."

He dialed and waited for an answer. "Yes. They've had me locked up. Apparently he tried to shoot the sheriff. I can? Good." He put the phone down. "I hope you're recording this," he said ominously.

"You know we are." Pete pointed to the camera mounted

on the wall.

Matt leaned forward. "Good. 'Cause you all are going to look like asses."

"We know that you were near the scenes of the murders." Pete started in the middle.

"I figured that out myself. My question is, how did you know where I was?"

"The sheriff and Deputy Macklin had reason to be suspicious of your activities and so they had a tracking device installed on your laptop."

"I see."

"What were you doing?"

"I've been given permission to tell you that for the last month or so I've been working as an informant for the DEA."

"What?!" I blurted out. Both Pete and Matt gave me dirty looks. I held up my hands and sat back in my chair.

"The DEA got a tip that there were some deputies helping the Thompsons import and deal drugs in the county. I'd already gone through the agency's interview process and they were ready to hire me. But they decided I should stay here a bit longer so I could help them ferret out the bad cops and get the information necessary to pull down the Thompsons," Matt said with a satisfied smirk on his face. I felt like my head was going to explode.

"No one here at the sheriff's office knew about this?" Pete asked.

"No. We had no idea which, or even how many, of the deputies were involved. For all we knew, the sheriff himself might be implicated." I felt my face turn red. "It wouldn't be the first time that a sheriff was involved in illegal activities in his county."

I couldn't contain myself. "You couldn't have told me this this morning?" I yelled.

"What part of being undercover don't you understand? If you'd let me make a call, I would have tried to get permission to tell you. But you wouldn't."

"If you can't sit there without talking, I'll have to ask you to leave," Pete told me. I looked at him, thinking he was kidding. He wasn't. I clamped my mouth shut and sat back.

"It became pretty obvious that Edwards was involved. He was one of the smartest officers on the force. I figured he must have some reason for staying. Turns out he likes to party. His habit isn't out of control, at least not physically, but mentally he's addicted to the thrills."

"Why didn't you step in when Nichols killed Ayers?"

"Actually, all of that happened too fast. By the time I realized what Nichols was doing, it was over. I wanted to step in and arrest him for the murders, but the guys at the DEA wanted me to hang back and continue to gather information. They were more interested in cleaning up the sheriff's office and bringing down the Thompsons. Arresting Nichols might or might not have accomplished those goals."

"But they're okay with you telling us all of this now?"

"Yes. They have enough to charge the Thompsons with a laundry list of crimes. With all of this coming out, they're probably raiding the Thompsons right now."

I didn't want to believe it. If what he said was true, then I had to give up everything I thought I'd discovered during the last month. Then something else dawned on me. I took a piece of paper and wrote a question, handing it to Pete.

Pete looked at the note and turned to Matt. "Did you realize that your investigations into the Thompsons were causing them to be hyper-paranoid?"

"I may have been noticed a few times. But paranoia is part of the drug trade. It never hurts to have to them off balance."

Did you pick up that pearl of wisdom from the DEA? I wanted to spit at him. His monkeying around was the catalyst for everything. I grabbed another piece of paper and started scrawling. I thrust it off to Pete when I was done.

"The reason they killed Ayers and the girl was to make my da... the sheriff look bad, to get him off their backs because they thought that he was putting pressure on them.

When in reality you were putting pressure on them." Pete finished reading the hastily written and grammatically challenged message.

"You can't blame me for the actions of criminals," Matt said, looking at me. "And maybe if your dad had focused on them earlier, it wouldn't have gotten to this point."

I could see Pete bowing up. "To be fair, the sheriff has tried to take them down several times over the last couple of years, but we know now that they had insider knowledge that kept him from catching them with the goods."

"And he should have known there were leaks," Matt said, focusing now on Pete.

Pete went over more details with Matt, but my mind was on fire. I couldn't concentrate. How could I have gotten everything so wrong? Some things were much clearer now, though. Like that whole weird conversation Matt and I had had about the black man murdered on the street corner.

"So Nichols or Edwards shot the man on the corner that you asked me about?" I said in a calm voice. Matt and Pete both looked at me, but didn't tell me to shut up.

"I'm pretty sure. But I couldn't get Dud to identify them."

"Why'd you ask me about it?"

He shrugged. "Fishing. I wanted to see how you'd react. Honestly, I'd noticed you acting squirrelly the last couple of weeks. I thought there was a chance you were involved," Matt said matter-of-factly.

I held my tongue, but I would have paid someone a thousand dollars for the privilege of slugging him in the face.

"And when we called in the FDLE?" I asked, grinding my teeth.

"The DEA pulled rank on them," Matt said smugly. *Great*, I thought, *the FDLE agents knew when they were collecting the files that they weren't going to do anything with them.*

Finally the interview was done. As he was walking out the door, Matt stopped. "You can tell your father that he'll have my resignation Monday morning."

Oh, the irony!

Pete's phone rang. After some back and forth he hung up. "They've processed Edwards. I told them to bring him up here to the interrogation room. Technically, I should probably call Maxwell, since I'm going to try and cover some of the Nichols murder too. But to hell with him."

There was a knock on the door ten minutes later and two deputies who regularly worked the jail led Edwards in. It was odd. He didn't look like the Edwards I'd known. Clearly it *was* him, but something seemed different. How much of it was real change and how much of it was my perception of him, I'm not sure. He still wore his uniform, but someone had removed all of the rank, patches and insignia from his shirt. The two deputies pushed him down into the chair and fastened his handcuffs through a bar on the table. No one spoke.

"If you all don't mind waiting outside," Pete said.

Pete took a minute to look Edwards over. Then he said, "We were friends. If you were in trouble, you could have come to us. Everyone here liked you."

"I guess," Edwards said, looking down at the table. "Do you even know anything about me?" he asked, looking at both of us.

"I do," Pete said. "I know you went to college at Florida State. You've had girlfriends, but never married. You write the best reports in the whole department. I also know that I invited you over to my house at least a dozen times during the last five years, and you never came over once."

"They were parties. You invited everyone."

"That's how you get to know people. So why don't you tell me about yourself? What was this all about?"

"I want a lawyer," Edwards spat out petulantly.

"No, you don't," Pete told him.

"I do."

"No. If you wanted a lawyer, you wouldn't have even started this conversation. You want to tell us why you did this. Otherwise, the word's going to go around the county that you're just another nut job working for Justin Thompson."

"I'm not working for him."

"He's not paying you?"

Silence from Edwards.

"Drugs, gambling, women?"

More silence.

"Fine." Pete stood up and started gathering his papers together. "But if you think you're going to get any protection or reward from the Thompsons, you should know that the DEA is in the process of raiding their homes, businesses and offices right now. And your opportunity to look cooperative is fading fast."

Pete paused to give Edwards a chance to answer. I didn't think he was going to, but just as Pete was turning to me, Edwards looked up.

"You know I can't get a real deal."

"If by 'real deal' you mean a deal where you walk or you do ten years, yeah, you're right. But maybe you can get a deal where you do twenty or twenty-five rather than life or life-plus."

"I want to see something in writing. Oh, yeah, any deal has to include federal charges. The DEA ought to be interested in what I can tell them concerning drugs and the Thompsons." Edwards looked at us with dead eyes.

"You talk to us first. We need to know what you're selling."

"In writing first." He made writing motions with his fingers.

Pete tried to pry him open, but he kept getting the same response.

"We'll see what we can do," Pete told him, then threw in, "Wait here," to goad him a little.

"I want to call my lawyer too. He'll need to look over the deal," Edwards shouted as Pete and I walked out the door.

CHAPTER THIRTY

An hour later we had a deal in writing, of sorts. Promises to only prosecute certain charges and to combine others. It was tricky because of Florida's mandatory minimum sentencing laws. Personally, I would have been glad to see him go to prison for the rest of his life, but if we wanted to clean out all the dirty cupboards we'd have to shoot him a straight deal. He was too savvy when it came to the law to be fooled.

At last everything was signed, sealed and delivered. We were once again sitting in the interrogation room with Edwards, only now we were joined by his lawyer, Chief Maxwell and Matt's supervisor from the DEA.

We were given the first crack at him. After the preliminaries of when and how he started working for the Thompsons, Pete moved on to the murders.

"You said you just craved a more exciting lifestyle, which included drugs, gambling and women. After you were substantially in debt to the Thompsons, they approached you."

"That's right. I started doing security on their drug runs and covering stuff up at the department, as well as informing them of any stings or ongoing investigations."

"When did Nichols get involved?"

"A year ago, maybe a little longer. I needed help. I was afraid I was going to get caught if I didn't have someone else in the department. Having him on board allowed us to cover for each other."

"Did you recruit him?" Pete asked.

Edwards laughed. "It wasn't hard. He was born to it. As soon as I took him to a couple of parties, he wanted more and more. At that point I just explained how it would work and he jumped onto the train. He wanted it all."

"What led up to the murder of Angie Maitland and Jeffrey Ayers?"

"All I can tell you is that the Thompsons started getting screwier than usual. Particularly paranoid when it came to Sheriff Macklin."

"Did you know that Matt Greene was working for the DEA and investigating the Thompsons?"

Edwards jerked upright in his chair, his eyes bright for the first time since he was brought in.

"No shit! Wow. That explains a few things."

"Like what?"

"Well, I saw him a couple of times driving around odd places at odd times. But he's such a weird guy I just put it down to him doing his own thing. Never tagged him as DEA. Wow! The Thompsons must have some real radar for snoops. I wish I'd known. I'd have rather tagged him than Nichols or your dad." He nodded to me. "Hell, I'd have rather popped that cold fish than Ayers." He sounded very sincere. I hoped Matt would get a chance to listen to these tapes someday.

"So the Thompsons were paranoid?" Pete made it a question, gently prodding Edwards.

"Yeah, they constantly wanted to know what the sheriff was doing. Always pissed if I couldn't give them anything. Justin and most of his lieutenants were constantly moving from one house to another. We knew that someone was watching us. I kept assuring them that it wasn't anyone from the sheriff's office, but they didn't believe me. In fact, they started searching me for a wire every time I talked with them. Wouldn't take my phone calls. On and on. Justin really had it in for the sheriff. He seemed sure that he was the problem.

"I think Nichols just got fed up hearing it, and one day he said, 'Why don't you get rid of him?' That's when things really got crazy. Justin was pretty sure he knew who was raping those women. He'd had problems with Conway and some of the girls at the club." Edwards got quiet for a moment.

"How did they get from there to framing Ayers?"

"That was Nichols. Nichols really wanted to be tight with the Thompsons. When the sheriff let Ayers go, Nichols told the Thompsons how most of the county thought that the sheriff had made a huge mistake and that they should exploit the situation. Honestly, I was surprised that Daniel Thompson went along with it. The old man didn't like Nichols that much. But like I said, the Thompsons were a lot crazier by that point. They thought the cops were going to raid them any minute. And, honestly, Justin's the one who really runs the whole operation these days. His father's what, seventy-six?"

"Who killed the girl?"

"I did. Nichols was supposed to. He was there, but he chickened out at the last minute. Nichols didn't have any problem getting her into his car. He pulled up alongside the bank, out of range of the camera, and he just called her over to his patrol car. Actually, Angie was his second attempt. He let the first woman go. So this time I was watching him. When I saw that he was chickening out, I did it for him," Edwards said cockily. He had an awful lot of faith in the plea bargain agreement.

Pete made a note. I knew he'd want to come back and get all the details on Angie's murder later, but right now it was important to get the broad strokes down on tape.

"Who set up Ayers?"

"Surprise, surprise, Nichols stepped up to the plate for

that one. Nichols pulled Ayers over. He'd been watching him. While he did that, I set up the scene in the back of the store with the woman's body. Lights off so no one would see me. Nichols came around with his lights on like an idiot, that's how the snoopy neighbor saw him. The rest was easy. Nichols didn't seem to mind shooting a man. Strangling a woman was too much for him, but not shooting Ayers."

"Who killed Conway?"

"Both of us were there. That was easy. We gave him some heroin and within an hour all we had to do was push his head underwater to make sure he was dead."

Pete couldn't resist a jab at Edwards's ego. "So why weren't you all smart enough to get him to give up his souvenirs?"

"Who would have thought he was dumb enough to keep that stuff at his parents' house?"

"So why'd you kill Nichols?" Pete asked.

"That's his fault." Edwards nodded toward me.

"How's that?" I couldn't keep myself from injecting.

"You called me and said that you were going to meet with Nichols and wanted me on stand-by. It didn't take a genius. I figured he wanted to make a deal and was using you, the sheriff's son and a member of the investigation, as a sounding board. I did what I needed to do. I got there before you. Wasn't that hard. Forced his gun into his mouth and pulled the trigger."

I felt a chill go over me. I wasn't sure if it was from listening to this cold-blooded killer, who I'd actually liked, or from the thought that my actions had led to him killing Nichols. Probably both.

"Of course, everything snowballed from there. The Thompsons went bat-shit crazy that I'd killed Nichols without asking them first. Talk about control freaks. Their paranoia was ratcheted up another notch, which I didn't even believe was possible. I saw the way they were looking at me. The old man, Daniel, was ready to cut me loose. And the only way that was going to happen was with me dead. So

I told them I'd solve everything once and for all." There was a brief pause as though he was trying for dramatic affect. "I'd kill Sheriff Macklin."

"How'd you think you'd get away with it?" Pete was genuinely interested.

"I thought that was pretty obvious." Edwards looked around at everyone. then he smiled. "You all haven't found the body yet."

We all looked at each other nervously. As if on cue, there was an insistent knock at the door. Pete got up and answered it. He stepped out for a minute and then came back in, looking grim.

"They found the body of Rufus Brinkman with a bullet in his chest about a block from the shooting," Pete told the room.

"There's your answer." Edwards looked proud.

"You were going to pin it on Mr. Brinkman."

"Yep. He made threats toward the sheriff about a month ago after a court case that went against his brother. I figured it would be easy to pin the shooting on him. I got an old hunting rifle from the Thompsons, then stopped Brinkman this morning and asked him if he had ever seen the rifle. I handed it to him to get his prints on it, then tied him up and put him in the trunk of my car.

"Again you," he nodded to me, "were very helpful. I wasn't sure how I was going to get away from Matt Greene, who'd managed to assign himself to my post during the parade. But, conveniently, you took him away." I wanted to slap the smug smile off his face. "I knew roughly when you all would be coming by in the parade, so I drove a block away and shot Brinkman and got back in time to shoot the sheriff. Unfortunately, that woman ran out into the parade. Who the hell was that, anyway?" Edwards asked.

I had begun to suspect who she was and, if I was right, I was going to have a pretty heavy debt to pay off.

The interview went on for hours as Pete, and later Chief Maxwell, the DEA supervisor and others questioned every detail. Turned out that Edwards had some bad news for Maxwell as well. One of his officers was also helping the Thompsons. It was a bit of luck for Dad. Maxwell wouldn't be able to use much of this against him in the election. But that was the only bright spot. I sat there wondering if Dad would come out of this looking okay, or if my bungling had not only led to several murders, but also to his electoral defeat in the fall.

Toward the end of the interview, Dad came into the room. For a moment he locked eyes with Edwards. I'm surprised the man's head didn't burst into flame from the heat of the anger that Dad shot at him. Dad walked stiffly to a chair, but seemed to change his mind and just stood there as the interview was completed. After Edwards was led out, there was a brief discussion about jurisdictions and prosecutions. Dad never met my eyes.

When we came out of the interview room, everyone was quiet. Normally, when you've gotten a solid confession to a major crime there are back slaps, high fives and invitations to get a drink, but not this time. Too much had gone wrong.

"Do you need me to drive you home or help with anything?" I asked Dad after everyone had left.

"No, I'm fine," he said curtly.

I wanted to apologize, but he clearly didn't want to talk to me right then, which I understood. I called Cara and followed up on the text I'd sent her right after the shooting. She'd been at the other end of the parade, so she hadn't seen any of it. I promised to talk with her tomorrow.

CHAPTER THIRTY-ONE

Sunday may have been a new day, but I didn't feel like I was facing a new world. I was dreading everything—the job of cleaning up all the reports and papers, facing up to my numerous screw-ups, and talking to Dad, who I knew blamed me for a lot of what had happened.

I lingered over my morning cereal with Ivy, delaying the point when I needed to go into the office. I was rinsing out my bowl at the sink when I heard a knock on the door. It was Cara and Alvin.

"I didn't want to give you a chance to say no," she said when I opened the door.

"I'm glad you're here." And I meant it. She gave me a big hug. Alvin bumped my leg and demanded a proper greeting. I leaned down and petted the Pug, who panted and puffed happily.

"Why don't we take a walk?" I suggested. It was a bit warmer today and the sun was bright.

We took a path I'd cut through the woods, Alvin trotting happily ahead of us and sniffing everything in sight. As we walked, I told her everything that had happened.

"I'm going into work today," I said.

"Shouldn't you take the day off?"

"I want to get most of my paperwork in order without having to deal with everyone else."

"They aren't going to blame you for what Nichols and Edwards did."

"Once the whole story comes out, it's going to be pretty obvious that lot of what happened was the result of my mistakes. I screwed this up right from the beginning. I never liked Matt, and I let that color everything I've done during the last couple of months. And if I hadn't been so focused on him, I might have figured out who the real bad cops were."

"You're being too hard on yourself."

"No harder than Dad's going to be. And for once I think he's right. I've done a lot of damage." I was getting madder and madder at myself. I'd tried not to think about it during the last twenty-four hours, but now everything was falling down around me and I only had one person to blame.

"It's okay. Everyone will understand. You've told me yourself that no one likes Matt."

"But I got it into my head that he was the mole and then used my relationship with my father to drag him into it. If I hadn't been his son, do you think he would have given my weak evidence and ideas so much credence?"

I couldn't believe how blind I'd been. What was crystal clear now was that I was a menace to Dad and the department. "I never should have become a deputy."

Cara tried to put her arm around me, but I turned away.

"I'm going to quit. I've done enough damage. It's time for me to find my own way in a career I'm more suited to."

"You know I've never been thrilled that you're a deputy, but I don't think you should quit like this. Give it some time," Cara counseled.

"That's just putting off the inevitable. I'm going into work and finish up what I can today. On Monday, I'll give Dad my resignation."

Having come to a decision, I hugged Cara and we headed back. Alvin had long tired of trying to track the beasts of the woods and panted along behind us.

Pete was at his desk when I got to the office. We greeted each other with grim nods.

"Not our finest hour," Pete said.

"No reflection on you. I'm the one that led my father down the wrong path."

"The only thing I blame you for is not telling me your suspicions about Matt." He held up his hand. "I know Matt and I have a history, but you should have trusted me." He was clearly hurt, and he was right.

"Another thing I did wrong."

"I'm not piling on. Just saying, next time have a little faith in me."

I didn't tell him that there wouldn't be a next time. I knew Pete would try to argue me out of it and I didn't have enough energy to fight him.

That afternoon we went around to Ayers's house and spoke with his mother and brother. They'd just come from church. She was wearing a dark green dress, and he looked lost in an off-the-rack suit. But he was clean and sober. They listened to us with dead eyes as we explained what we could about the circumstances surrounding their son and brother's murder. Mrs. Ayers thanked us with a heavy heart, while Wayne just nodded to us and wiped tears from his eyes.

We drove to Angie Maitland's house next. Allen Maitland answered the door, his eyes shaded by dark rings.

"Nothing you can say will make it better," he told us and slammed the door.

I offered to start down the list of rape victims, but Pete told me he'd talk to them on Monday.

My phone rang as I was finishing up my report on the Edwards interview. It was Eddie.

"I saved your dad's life and you don't even call and say thanks." He still sounded excited.

"Nice dress."

"Thanks. That was the first time I've worn it in public. I'm hoping no one recognized me. I'm standing out pretty bad as it is since the Feds came in and took almost everyone else in. I look like the last man standing."

"That's what you wanted, isn't it?" I was grateful to him, but I wasn't really in the mood to chat.

"Yes. But, of course, Mom said that they're going to make bail this week, so who knows what will happen after that. I might have to take a trip. Maybe I'll go down to Miami."

"You would probably like Miami," I said, halfway serious.

"Sorry I didn't get there sooner. But after I called you yesterday morning, I heard Dad and the Chief talking. I got enough of what they were saying to figure some things out and came down to the parade to make sure you'd really gotten the guy. Then I saw that deputy and he had a hunting rifle. Everything just clicked." Eddie was excited.

I was glad someone was proud of their part in all of this. I think Eddie was the only one.

"I'm glad you were there." I did owe him some gratitude.

"Gave me a chance to dress out. I finally found an advantage to being a cross-dresser. All those years of dressing up and practicing in heels." He was proud.

"I do appreciate the chance you took."

"I know my family's hurt a lot of people. I just wanted to balance the scales a little bit."

"If you need some money to get out of town, let me know." It wasn't his fault that I didn't do a better job with his information.

"Thanks. I'll just have to see how things go." That was the first time he hadn't grabbed at money I'd offered.

I got to work early on Monday and typed and printed my resignation letter. In it I took full blame for the fiasco that had resulted from my investigation of Matt Greene, who turned out to be working for the DEA, and my failure to search for other suspects.

The atmosphere in the office was grim. No matter how you looked at it, we'd lost two deputies in a week. Most people were having a hard time getting their minds around the idea that both Nichols and Edwards were a pair of vipers. And what made it was worse was that one of them was dead and they didn't have the chance to show him how much they hated him. In fact, Nichols would never officially be guilty of anything.

As I walked toward Dad's office, I realized I'd never heard the building so quiet on a Monday morning. His assistant barely gave me a glance as I by passed her desk. A bark answered my knock at the door.

Dad sat at his desk with Mauser on the floor beside him, looking up to see who was coming through the door.

"I brought Mauser in to cheer people up," Dad said, but I knew that he'd really brought the Great Dane in to cheer himself up. Mauser had clearly picked up on the mood and didn't even get up to greet me. Instead he sighed heavily and put his head back down on his paws.

I handed Dad the envelope with my resignation.

"What's this?" he asked. His voice had a hard edge to it.

"My resignation."

He started to say something, but apparently thought better of it and closed his mouth. Composing himself, he finally said, "You don't have to do this."

"I screwed up. It cost people their lives. I think I do."

"I'm not going to pretend that I'm happy with the job you did on this case. Particularly where it concerns Matt. But I share a lot of the blame. I'm your boss. I'm the one that should have forced you to look deeper and question your own assumptions. Do you think *I* should resign?"

His tack took me by surprise and I had to think a minute before answering.

"No, you trusted my judgment and I'm the one that failed. I've never been a good deputy."

"You've never been like all the other deputies. That's not

the same thing. I'm not going to fight with you about this. But Edwards's case and the prosecution of the Thompsons are going to take years. I want you to remain as a reserve officer for now. That way you can continue to work on the case when needed, and when you go to court and testify you can wear your uniform. See this through." His eyes were locked on mine. I didn't have much of an option.

"Fair enough," I said and he put the resignation in his in-box.

"I'll get HR to do the paperwork this afternoon. We'll make it official the end of January," he said dismissively.

As I walked out of his office I thought, *Now what?*

Larry Macklin returns in:

February's Regrets
A Larry Macklin Mystery–Book 4

Here's a preview:

I looked out the window onto my frozen twenty acres and thought, *Could there be a worse month to be unemployed than February?* All I wanted to do was crawl back into bed. Ivy, my adopted tabby cat, looked at me as though she thought anyone who got out of bed to do anything but eat and do their business was an idiot. She was enjoying my unemployment and thought I should just spend every day scratching her and dispensing treats.

"Not this morning, girlie. I need to find a real job to keep us in frosted flakes and cat food." She mewed and rubbed against me. "Enjoy," I said, pushing my cereal bowl over to her so that she could lick the last bit of milk from the bottom.

While it had been almost a month since I had handed in my resignation, it had only been a week since my last day working full time for the Adams County Sheriff's Office. It had taken that long to finish up the paperwork on the murders, rapes and attempted killing of the sheriff that had led me to hand in my notice. It hadn't helped that we'd been assisted by the Florida Department of Law Enforcement and the Drug Enforcement Agency, adding untold levels of bureaucracy to the reports.

At the request of the sheriff, who also happened to be my father, I was still a reserve deputy with the department, but I didn't plan on working any more hours than necessary to maintain that status. All of which begged the question of what I was going to do now.

At least the sun was out, giving me enough motivation to

push back from the kitchen table and get dressed. I'd just managed to put on pants and a shirt when there was a knock at the front door. Since my property was about five miles from town, it was odd that someone would be visiting me out of the blue on a Tuesday morning. *Jehovah's Witnesses or Baptists?* I wondered as I went to the door.

"Hey there, Mr. Brighteyes," Shantel Williams said when I opened the door. Shantel was one of the best crime scene techs in the department and a friend.

"What are you doing here?" I asked, surprised.

"Freezing my patootie off. You going to invite me in?" Her smile was forced. Normally she was the type of person who was always on the verge of laughter, but she seemed distracted this morning.

"Yeah, yeah, come in."

She followed me into the living room and I suddenly noticed how filthy the place was.

"I see you're settling into unemployment," she teased, but again the humor seemed more out of habit than part of her normal good spirits.

"Are you okay?" I asked, concerned.

"Let me sit down." She took a seat on the sofa, shifting a pile of books out of her way.

Shantel had only been out to my place once before, to drop me off when my car was in the garage, so I knew she was there for a reason. I had to resist the urge to bombard her with questions, giving her time to get her thoughts together.

"I need your help." Before she could stop it, a tear rolled down her dark brown cheek. She wiped it away in irritation.

"Anything," I said and meant it. When I'd gone to work for the sheriff's office, Shantel had been quick to give me advice and to help me learn how to preserve and search a crime scene. Once I became an investigator, I quickly learned that Shantel and her partner, Marcus Brown, were the best assets I had in the field. Not that Shantel wasn't quick to let me know if I did something stupid. She did that with everyone and didn't care who she might piss off. She wouldn't tolerate fools.

"My niece, Tonya, is missing."

I remembered seeing a couple pictures on her desk. One of them was of a smiling, lanky woman in a graduation gown.

"From Adams County?"

"Yeah. She lives over on King Street and people saw her Saturday night. But she's just gone. She texts me every day. Dumb stuff, but every day. Nothing since Saturday."

I'd never seen Shantel this rattled. Usually she was the boss in any room. If I had been the type to give hugs easily I would have gone over to her, but I wasn't so I just sat across from her, feeling helpless.

"Have you talked with anyone at the department?"

I saw a spark of the old Shantel when she gave me a look that was a mix of irritation and frustration. "Of course I talked to Pete. But you know we're four deputies short. Your father's going crazy because he can't afford the overtime." She threw me an accusing look, then went on. "Pete took all the information, but he's got a pile of cases on his desk. And... Tonya's life has been a bit mixed up since she graduated from high school."

"How old is she?"

"Twenty. She got into some trouble when she went to community college in Tallahassee. Partying too much. It got a little scary, but I went and brought her home. She's been doing well since then. Can't get a job, but no more drugs or alcohol."

"You know I quit."

"I know you're still a reserve deputy. And you're the best investigator we have... had."

I was pretty sure she was just flattering me to get some help.

"I..."

"Your dad will let you take the case if you ask."

That was a conversation I didn't really want to have.

"Before we do anything desperate like talk to my father, let me look into it. Maybe there's a simple explanation. Did you take the day off?"

"I couldn't go to work today. I drove around most of last night looking for her car. I've worked for the department for fifteen years... I know that people go missing all the time and show back up. People do weird crap that their families never thought they'd do. I *know* that. And I pray that's the case here. But I'm scared." She dropped her gaze to the floor.

"Something else is going on. What do you know?"

Shantel sighed. "I know something I shouldn't."

I just looked at her, puzzled.

"I was over in Tallahassee last week and stopped by to see a friend at the sheriff's office there. I'm not saying who 'cause it wasn't their fault. I was in their office and they left to take care of some business. I was bored and there was a file on the desk. I admit it. I'm a snoop sometimes. I got to looking at it." She just stopped talking.

"What was in it?" I prompted.

"You can't tell anyone I told you this."

"What?"

"Promise. 'Cause if it got around, my friend could be fired."

"I promise," I said, a bit exasperated. "Now what did you see?"

Shantel sighed heavily. "I'm probably worrying for no reason. But..." She paused for so long that I thought I'd have to prod her again, but she finally went on. "The file was on a murder case that Leon County is investigating. When I opened it there was a picture of a young black girl, and she looked so much like Tonya that I almost dropped the thing."

"But this was before Tonya went missing?" I was a little confused. The fact that I was entertaining a visitor before ten o'clock in the morning wasn't helping.

"That's right. I looked at the file a lot closer then... This is the terrifying part. It's a Swamp Hacker case."

I felt my stomach heave and my breathing grew rapid. "Not possible. It must have been an old file… or someone's messing with you."

"They haven't made anything public yet. But I know what I saw. There were the cuts on the back. Just like…" Shantel stopped, near tears again. I'd never seen her this close to the edge. We'd worked a hundred accidents and murders together, including a gruesome body found in a hot tub the month before. She was always a rock of emotional stability when others were choked up or throwing up.

"And then Tonya went missing," I said for her.

She nodded. "You're the only one I've told about the Leon County case. Leaking information on an active murder case, even to you, is a crime. That kind of screw up could get me fired at the very least. I never should have been snooping," she chastised herself.

"Even if it is a new Hacker case, it can't have anything to do with Tonya."

"All of his victims came from here," Shantel reminded me.

"But only one of the bodies was found in Adams County," I said.

"Yeah, the rest were left in swamps in Leon or Jefferson County. You were how old back then?"

"Fifteen. You know, I saw Sierra Randal's body." My mind went back to that day in January sixteen years ago.

"How'd you manage that?"

"I was in high school and had joined the journalism club, so I was staying after a lot and didn't always come home on the bus. Dad picked me up that day. He'd just become an investigator in October. When he drove up in the unmarked car, I thought it was so cool… and funny as hell to see him working in a jacket and tie. Halfway home he got a call about a body that was found just inside the county line. Dad being Dad, he told me we were going to the scene. It was only his second murder investigation."

"Taking a boy to a murder scene," Shantel said, shaking

her head, but I knew she wasn't surprised. My father could be incredibly single-minded and a bit clueless.

"I was thrilled. I thought that this was my chance to be a real reporter. Of course, when we got there, Dad ordered me to stay in the car. We were parked about a quarter mile from the body. They'd already figured that this case was related to the others in Leon County and were determined to preserve any tire prints or other evidence the killer might have left behind."

"How long did you wait in the car?" she asked.

"About five minutes after Dad was out of sight. I followed the road up to where Dad and the other deputies were looking around for tracks and other obvious evidence. They were waiting on forensics and the sheriff. I don't know what the hell I thought I was doing, but I walked to the side of the dirt road. Everyone was looking at a spot about twenty feet on the other side of the ditch. The ground was wet and mucky. I remember it was warm for a winter's day."

"No one stopped you?"

"I just walked up like it was the most normal thing in the world for me to do. Most of them were too captivated by the body to notice me. Even from there you could see the horrible slashes across her back. I don't know what I imagined a dead body would look like, but this was horrible. I wanted to go help her. She looked so alone. I think I even started to move toward her, but then I felt a hand grab the back of my coat."

"Don't have to tell me who that was." Shantel smiled a little.

"He pulled me halfway back to the car. I heard words that he normally reserved for lawnmowers that wouldn't start."

Shantel shook her heard. "I didn't see my first murder victim until I was almost thirty."

"It definitely made an impression on me, but I think the weeks and months afterward when Dad was trying to find the killer made an even bigger impression. He was so intent on catching the Hacker that we hardly saw him for months. Of course, he had to spend a lot of time in Leon County with the task force, but it was more than that. I think he personally interviewed every witness in Adams County, and he sat in on most of the interviews in Leon too."

"The last body was found in April."

"Dad stayed on the case full time through the summer. When the sheriff reassigned him, Dad refused to quit and worked during his off hours for another couple of months before Mom convinced him that he had to let it go."

"I remember all us single girls being scared to death to be alone at night. Even if there were a couple of us, we'd get a guy we trusted to go with us if we were going out. And when they found the couple murdered in the swamp, I just refused to go anywhere at night for weeks. Guy or no guy," Shantel stated.

"Of course, none of the murders were actually committed in the swamp. I remember how mad Dad was every time a newspaper or TV reporter called the murderer the Swamp Hacker. He didn't even kill them by hacking them."

"That's right, he hit them on the head. Oh, my God." Shantel put her hand up to her mouth.

I realized I'd forgotten the reason Shantel came to me. "I'm sure Tonya is fine."

"Help me find her, Larry," she pleaded.

"I'll do what I can." I didn't believe that Tonya could be a victim of the Hacker. I didn't really believe that he could be back. If he was, it was going to be a shock to a lot of people. I had no idea how Dad would react. I wanted to give him a heads-up, but Shantel was right. She could have been fired for what she'd already done. The leak had to stop with us. The LCSO would have to give out the news soon enough. They couldn't sit on the story forever.

"What can we do?" Shantel seemed so lost. It was a reminder that even the strongest person can be dealt a body blow.

"First, let's forget the Leon County murder. Even if it is the same murderer, there's no evidence that it has anything to do with Tonya. We're just going to tackle this like we would any missing person."

"I've talked to everyone I can think of and I've been working on a timeline." Shantel seemed to get a little of her old determination back, pulling up the timeline on her phone.

"Great. I want to copy it and we'll start working on a plan for today," I said, getting up and digging for a notepad.

After making notes from the timeline, I asked, "This is Saturday. What did she do Friday?" I knew we'd have to work further and further back if we didn't hit on anything right away.

"She spent all day Friday looking for work. She'd had jobs in Tallahassee, several, when she was in college, but just entry-level stuff and, with her partying, she'd either quit or been let go after a couple of months. And, yes, I know how this sounds. But she was just like every other kid who goes to college, gets in over their head and flunks out the first year. She'd taken it to heart. Tonya really wants to make good. She's applied to just about every business here in the county."

"Must have been hard."

"She seemed okay. Maybe a little down, but determined."

"Does she have a boyfriend?"

"Nothing steady. She's only had one serious boyfriend, but he went to work out in North Dakota and she went to college. That's when they drifted apart. Since high school, she's just had a few guy friends, but nothing serious. I'd have known. There was nothing she liked better than telling me every detail of her social life. That girl can talk. If she went out on a date, I'd get a couple of pictures before it was even over. She did all that Twitter, Facebook and Snap-whatever stuff... But there's been nothing for days."

"What about her parents?"

"Tonya was raised by my momma. She's worried sick

too. But, honestly, Momma's pretty clueless. My sister died of a drug overdose ten years ago. She'd never taken care of Tonya. No idea who the daddy is."

I realized how little I knew of Shantel's life. I knew that most of her family lived in Adams County, though she'd spent part of her childhood in Savannah when her father was in the military. But I'd only recently learned that she'd been married and divorced. How can we work with people, call them our friends, and yet know so little about their real lives? I felt like I hadn't been much of a friend.

I stood up. "Let's split up and interview as many people as possible. Did Pete put out a BOLO on her car?"

"Oh, yeah. Pete knew he wasn't going to get rid of me without doing that at least." She shook her head. "The car has to be here some place. It's so old and broken down, I don't think it can make it out of the county."

ACKNOWLEDGMENTS

Thanks to everyone who has read this series so far—I am humbled by how well it has done and I'm glad that others seem to enjoy reading this series as much as I enjoy writing it.

A special thanks to Sam Azner for his speedy beta read of the manuscript.

As always, I have to recognize the amazing and constant support and encouragement I've received from H. Y. Hanna. Her advice has been invaluable and I firmly believe that her cover designs have played a big part in the series' success. Words cannot express my appreciation for all her help.

Good fortune smiled on me when I met a woman who could be my friend, my editor and my wife. Many things in my life, including this series, could not be accomplished without Melanie by my side.

Original Cover Design by H. Y. Hanna
Paperback Cover Design by Robin Ludwig Design Inc.
www.gobookcoverdesign.com

ABOUT THE AUTHOR

A. E. Howe lives and writes on a farm in the wilds of north Florida with his wife, horses and more cats than he can count. He received a degree in English Education from the University of Georgia and is a produced screenwriter and playwright. His first published book was *Broken State*; the Larry Macklin Mysteries is his first series and he has plans for more. Howe is also the co-host of the "Guns of Hollywood" podcast, part of the Firearms Radio Network. When not writing or podcasting, Howe enjoys riding, competitive shooting and working on the farm.

Made in United States
North Haven, CT
10 May 2023

36423059R00136